Fourteen Days
in Silicon Valley

William C. Sailor

A Money Bomb Press Book, Published by Lightning Source, a
subsidiary of Ingram Press Publishers
Money Bomb Press Books are available through Ingram Press, and
available for order through Ingram Press Catalogues

Visit me at https://www.facebook.com/WilliamSailorAuthor

Printed in the United States of America
First Printing: July 2015
Published by Sojourn Publishing, LLC

ISBN: 978-1-62747-141-1
Ebook ISBN: 978-1-62747-142-8

Acknowledgements

This book was written with the encouragement and wisdom provided by Tom Bird at Sojourn Publishing LLC. Elana Maloul served as an excellent editor and proofreader. Friends who helped me with the content of the book include Dan N., Neal M., and Tom G. The late Helen Schucman, the late Kenneth Wapnick and other miracle workers guided me with the conclusion. I also wish to thank my wife and fellow student Judith Horning Sailor for her beauty, patience and love.

Foreword

This book contains the continuing adventures of Stan Hall, who relies on old friends and family just to survive in California's prosperous and expensive Silicon Valley. He is also trying to make child-support payments to his ex-girlfriend for their son, of whom she has sole custody. The story takes a sinister turn shortly into the story, when there is a tragic death at the shop where Stan works.

This is not a disguised autobiography. It is not meant to be a Hero's Journey, nor a tragedy. It is also clear than Stan is no saint.

The characters that interact in this story come from a variety of social, economic, and cultural backgrounds. The main character does have some problems with race relations that he does not fully recognize. Those parts of the story may give the reader a few chuckles and a few shivers.

A reader who expects political or social judgments in the end may be disappointed. The book has no simple formula for change in our laws to make the world a fairer place. This author would rather heal himself first, and bring peace of mind to others. Changing the external world is only a distant priority.

Stan becomes very interested in philosophy for a brief period during the story and considers himself an amateur champion of a "new" philosophy. This philosophy is, of course, new only to him. The story conveys some discussion of competing philosophical propositions. If you wish to enjoy the story simply in that way, you are welcome to do so.

The 28-year-old main character also shows signs of paranoia, which is confirmed when he is placed in a psychiatric unit and given the diagnosis of "schizophrenia." His real insanity, however, is his practice of promoting resentment in himself and others, and hanging on to it as if it is a great, prized possession. The adventure he experiences is made entirely possible by his fear, distrust and loathing of humanity. He looks out and sees an insane world, but it is entirely a product of his insane mind. Once he sees the world differently, the world is saved.

Prologue by Stan's Father, Bill Hall

I t shocked me, to say the least, when Stan called me after having gone missing for over a week. The last time I had seen him before that he had attacked me, hitting me with a brick in my face. But I had no idea what he had been going through. The death of his mother happened right after he had lost a lifelong friend to an accident.

Stan had disappeared right after his mother Janis died. He had returned to the house to attack me, as if I had been the one who killed her - my wife of over thirty years. It was so worrisome to see him react to this tragedy in that way. I still think about her every day, and I miss her dearly. It is a consolation, I guess, that Stan and I are talking again, and he says he has stopped hating me. In fact, he keeps saying over and over again that he loves me.

I spend a lot of time going to AA meetings, both before and after work. My job is so lousy it barely pays for the gas to get there and back, but I am grateful for what I have. My AA friends are so kind to me. As I sit in this apartment, there are flowers surrounding me and comforting me in my grief. Several friends have written me notes and have stopped by.

Janis was the only love of my life. We met, fell in love, were married and had two children. The pressures of my job were incredible back in the 1980s, and I was drinking quite a bit. I got caught with booze on my breath at an executive meeting at Lockheed, where I had forgotten to bring my briefing materials with me. My career at that employer ended quickly, but soon a small startup company hired me. Things were really taking off in "The Valley" back then. They talked about a permanent shortage of people!

When Robert, my older son, was killed in a car crash, I could not bear the pain. Seeing what it did to my poor wife was pure torture. I could not do anything except drink – that is, when she threw me out of the house the first time. Come to think of it, that is when Stan started to treat me badly, too.

Our family had been reunited lately. This time I had stayed sober for eight consecutive weeks – but really the hardest part was the first few days. Janis let me move back into the house again. It was sort of agreed that I would not be bothering Stan too much. We did not see him too often, but when we did, he was always polite. He was very quiet too. He never had much to say.

Yes, Stan had not been doing too well lately. He had lost his career position at the Fairfield National Laboratory and had to work in a machine shop. I was so very proud of him, the way he had graduated from UC Berkeley, with honors, in chemical engineering. Those years of hard work he had put in at Berkeley. He was a chip off the old block, as they say. I am smiling as I write this. How could I smile when my beautiful wife is dead? She is never coming back. Never.

As I said, Stan went missing after he attacked me. I had reported him to the police, but of course I would not press charges. We had some friends in the Mountain View police department who I thought could help us –

that is, me – locate my son. We had known them for years. My wife had invited them over for pastries shortly after my older son Bob had died, and had stayed in contact ever since.

The fact that they could find Stan and help me to see him again has got to be the only bright side of the story of this family. Speaking of family, both of *my* parents are gone, and I sure miss them now. Both of my sisters died as children, from measles, of all things.

The police officers worked hard with our attorney Charles Schultz, to set up a situation for Stan where he could physically be under house arrest, yet live at home, and still keep the required 500 yards away from me. That meant that I had to get the apartment that I am staying in.

After Stan moved back into the house it was only a few days before he called me. Calling me on the phone is not a violation of his restraining order, so we talked for a while. He thanked me for working with the "cops" to get him home again. I would do anything for him.

Another day or two went by before he told me what really happened to him over those couple of weeks. He did not make himself out to be a victim or a hero. He just told me what happened, and it is a story of a remarkable downward spiral. Apparently it is my role to write down the story that he told me, just as he told it to me, so others can hear it too.

Wednesday, Day 1

I left Mom's house at 6 AM in Los Altos and was at the shop in Mountain View by 6:30. Getting started early is one way to beat the notoriously heavy traffic in Silicon Valley. My beautiful pickup truck had served me well over the years, and continued to work well. It was the only thing I owned that still functioned as it should.

It has been about six months since I started working as a "gopher" at the Kozy machine shop, having lost my position at Fairfield National Laboratory. "Kozy" is what we call the family that owns the shop, but their actual name is Kozumplick.

Curt would be at the shop by seven and I looked forward to enjoying some donuts with him. It did not really bother me that I had gained a few pounds since all that horrible stuff happened to me last year. Enjoying a few good bites of food was just about my only source of pleasure.

There is a large roll-up door in the back of the shop and I was the only one besides the Kozy brothers, Bart and Curt, who had a key. The door is quite heavy, and I could probably lift it more easily than either of them. That is probably why they hired me. Opening the shop is half of what I did there. Running errands was the other half.

When I unlocked the outer padlock, using the "Stanley One" key, it just fell to the ground – the lock, that is. Someone had cut it overnight. The second lock is the digital keypad under a metal plate, where the correct combination must be entered. It was untouched, and I opened it. The door rolled up as usual, and the smell of metal-cutting oil wafted out the way it did every other day. The lathes and other computer-controlled machines had rested during the night, and they would be busy soon, when the next workday started.

The padlock had probably been cut off the door ten times since I'd started working at the shop. No one had ever made it all the way into the shop, though.

In the back right corner of the shop, the panel on the large security box glowed light blue as it always does. I let my fingers key in the password from memory, then spun around and crossed a few feet of concrete floor to the breaker panel. Lights on. Again, my muscle memory was completely operational, and I walked to the coffee maker, pulled out yesterday's coffee and filter, and dumped it in the trash. I pulled out a new filter, placed it in the basket and poured in the coffee - Yuban, of course. We all have been drinking Yuban together since high school.

How ironic it was that when we were kids, *we* were the ones going out and cutting locks in the middle of the night. Back then, we drank Yuban in case our crime kept us out all night.

The shop is about 50 feet deep and about 60 feet wide. Our best machines, the computer-controlled Mazak FJV-20 vertical mills, were in a row in the front. Various smaller prototyping machines, such as manually controlled mills and lathes, were set into the back of the shop. They were not used very often anymore. One of those machines, a LeBlonde lathe, had been in the Kozys' garage since I was a kid living next door.

The Mazak FJV-20s could turn out about a thousand machine cuts per hour, which sometimes translated into twenty or more very elaborate pieces per hour. Their nickname was "matic," short for "automatic." The skilled craft workers who make the machines run are called "CNC programmers," where CNC stands for "Computer Numerical Controlled." In other words, machinists today are no longer really machinists; they are essentially a specialized type of computer programmer.

All machine work was awarded on competitive bid. This last year, the shop seemed to be doing very well, turning out as much as two thousand dollars per hour per machine. There was even talk of a graveyard shift with a second set of operators to turn out even more parts and more money.

Bart and Curt did have some peculiar ways about them. For instance, after winning a contract they would immediately begin paying the employees in advance for the work they would do: a full month's pay at a time. They said it kept the workers loyal and more amiable towards a slightly lower pay. They also had the peculiar idea that as little money as possible should be kept in the bank. I never asked for an explanation from them, but I did once heard Midge, their mother, say, "Can't trust those Jewish bankers."

She would be coming in later that day, probably to bring in lunch.

I had come to know and almost be a part of this fine, if eccentric, family. We had lived next door to them when I was just a little boy. Bart and I went to elementary school together. We used to race our bicycles in the dirt, making growling sounds out of our mouths as if we were riding motorcycles. We were always very serious. Later, in middle school, we rode actual motorcycles in the dirt, trying our best to act like racers. Curt had a mini-bike by then and would ride double on the thing with his friend Rudy.

It seemed like those days went on forever and ever.

The family also included two older boys: Mark and Bruce. I had always hated Bruce, the oldest one, even though I admired him because he had such cool motorcycles and many girlfriends, and starred on the basketball team. But he always called me "fatso" and put me down. It is hard to find words to explain how I feel about Mark. He began as someone I could always count on, until he turned on me and got me fired from my job at Fairfield. He ruined my career when he took his brother Bruce's side against me in the whistleblower case.

Then there was Midge, or Mrs. Kozumplick, who would give long lectures on the Bible and the never-ending struggle between God and Satan: how we all have to choose one side or the other. At the shop, her role has been mostly to provide lunch for us in the middle of the day. She also helps with the bookkeeping. And she still provides us with Bible lectures.

The front left corner of the shop had a small office containing a desk with a computer, a set of file cabinets, and another table for the coffee maker. I sat at that table with my donuts. In the corner of the office was a safe with a dial combination lock. That is where the company's money was kept, never at the bank.

Curt pulled into the front of the shop at seven, as usual, and gave his big smile and friendly hello. "Hey partner, long time no see." I then gave my usual reply, "Yeah, about 12 hours," with a small chuckle. "Donut?" I offered. "Nah, not now," he said, walking right over to one of the CNC machines. "We have to catch up from yesterday because Rudy had to leave early."

I hadn't noticed until then that there was a line of about fifty unfinished parts on a bench near the machine. Rudy *had* said he was feeling sick.

Curt looked over his shoulder. "Power is good?" he asked. I had indeed reset all the breakers this morning and we were ready to go. The machine is operated through a keypad like a computer, and it also has a small TV screen like a computer. Curt carefully followed the instructions on the screen, dialing in the morning calibrations. Even though the machine is called a "fully automatic," a hand-held micrometer is still required for calibration every half-day of operation.

I kept a safe distance from him while I watched. Sometimes the machines randomly spray out some oil and I didn't want any getting on my donut. "What did he say he was sick with?" I asked. "I don't know, probably love-sick again over what's-her-name," said Curt. "I used to kind of like her, but not so much anymore since she started using dope," I said. "Yeah, I don't have too much use for dopers either," said Curt.

We were talking about Rudy's girlfriend, about 21, named Brendalyn.

The production run of the last 50 parts from yesterday was running by 7:30. Curt was an incredibly good machinist now, at age 27. He probably could be making quite a bit of money relatively risk-free at any large company, but he was dedicated to the family business.

As I mentioned before, the business had been doing quite well lately. Its main source of revenue was parts produced for defense contractors who did not want to keep all their capability in-house. So we were able to get lucrative jobs from Varian, Fairchild, Teledyne and Lockheed when defense spending was on an upswing. Apparently, it had lately been on an upswing.

Bart arrived before eight and he had Midge with him, which was unusual. Midge walked right up to me. "Hi Stan" she said, like I was one of her kids. "Hi," I said, somewhat startled. She poured a cup of coffee for Bart, who was walking in with a briefcase and a smile. "Hello Mr. Hall," he said.

Bart put the briefcase down in the office on the table next to the coffee maker, opened it up and started poring through it. Since he seemed a little preoccupied, as he often is, I walked over to where he was and checked in on him. One of the few positive contributions that I could make at the machine shop was to provide some math or computing advice when there was some sort of calculation to be done, so I stood at the ready, just in case.

Midge was talking to Curt in the front part of the shop. After a few minutes, they both headed into the office to join Bart and me. Midge said, "Stan, have you heard the news?" "No, heard what news?" "Bruce is going to be on the TV this morning at 8:00. He will be on with the President of the United States." I could not believe what I was hearing. Bruce was the oldest of the four boys and had been at Fairfield Lab for about five years, after getting his PhD from Princeton in physics, and working at Stanford for a while. Bruce had been the one to get me thrown out of Fairfield Lab, and Midge and the family all knew that.

Mark, the second-oldest boy, had been working with me on a much-publicized program that was at the heart of the future of the Laboratory. I had found some technical flaws in the program "The Advanced Tunneling Underground Munition," and had brought it to Bruce's attention. Bruce expressed nothing but scorn for my observation, and he claimed that there was no funding available to study the defect or ways of working around the problem. When I finally went to the Inspector General of the US Department of Energy, a couple of heads rolled. Foolishly, I had not predicted that one of the heads to be metaphorically "cut off" would be my own. Bruce, who survived the purge, orchestrated a campaign to brand me as some sort of a threat to national security. He painted me as a criminal because I had been drunk driving while still at Berkeley and had never reported it to the Office of Personnel Management. All this, despite the fact that I had quit drinking before I even came to work at the Lab.

7

The key witness against me, I suspect, was Mark Kozumplick, who received an unexpected promotion after I was fired. My termination papers said that I was discharged for alcohol abuse, yet I had never had a drink while working there.

For a while, it seemed I was unemployable by anyone. The Kozys were the only ones to give me a job.

I felt a drop of sweat running down my brow. It was quite early in the morning to be sweating so much already. It was eight o'clock, and Bart had turned on "Channel 7 Morning News."

The newscaster, Monica Trujillo, announced that the President of the United States had made a brief visit to Fairfield National Laboratory and that some videotape of last night's event would be up soon. I sat down and had another donut, which was gone by the time the film clip came on.

The picture that came on the little 20" TV was that of the President shaking the hand of the director of the Laboratory, David Plaque, who was standing to the right of the President, while the deputy director stood to the left of the President. The deputy director was Bruce. The President was there, according to the report, to congratulate the Lab on their completion of the new, large, computing cluster, which had already tested as the "speediest computer currently in the world."

When I looked over at Midge, she was smiling broadly. I asked, with a quiver in my voice, "He got another promotion?" She nodded her head. I was astonished, not so much at the promotion, but at the fact that Midge approved of the situation.

She knew all about how Bruce had lived his life. By the time he was in sixth grade he was the schoolyard bully. In high school, he had spent almost all his time stealing expensive cars and motorcycles for a profit — until he got caught, that is. That's when he had to go to a Juvenile Delinquency camp in Montana for a year to be "rehabilitated." He returned from camp shooting heroin, and when Midge tried to get him to stop he had beaten her badly, sending her to the emergency room. After leaving the house, he lived in a shed behind his girlfriend's house, became some sort of home-schooled lawyer and was able to have his crime record sealed. The only reason he was able to get into Princeton was because of a basketball scholarship.

Her explanation for Bruce's behavior only a few months ago, when I got fired from Fairfield, was that her son had renounced God and had gone over to the side of Satan. She had been in prayer for him, waiting for the day when he would recognize the madness in his life and come back to God. However, it looked to me like his "madness" had paid off quite well lately, seeing as a Deputy Director position comes with a salary of almost a half-million dollars a year.

I tried to look at Midge as she smiled at the TV, but I could not stand it and had to walk away. I found a better place to be, over near the matic, which Curt had set running earlier that morning. I verified that, yes, indeed, the parts were coming out perfectly, just the way they should.

Three other machinists had begun their shifts by then, and had begun setting up their matics for work.

The three were Josh, Seth and Rudy. Rudy, the one who had had to leave work early the day before, was the same Rudy who used to ride on the back of Curt's mini-bike when we were in middle school.

"Hey Rudy, feeling better?" I asked with a somewhat playful tone. He was just staring at his machine. "Hi Stan, how are you?" His tone was flat. "How is Brendalyn" I asked him. There was no answer. I walked away because it was time for me to check the ordering sheets.

Ordering sheets are the old-school way of keeping track of which supplies are needed. For instance, our machines use a lot of cutting oil, which we buy in 55-gallon drums. When we start to run low, a request is put on the ordering sheet. Most often I need to get cutting tools for the automatic machines, which will break a tool during a run probably once per day. We always keep plenty of extra tools, but the supply can run low. I wanted to take care of a supply run that morning because time would be a little tight in the afternoon due to the doctor's appointment I had at two o'clock. I also had to do a delivery of the final 50 pieces of the most recent job by five o'clock.

I spent some time reconciling the order sheets. When the sheets were done, I got into the company van and was completely overcome with grief. I had lost everything by telling the truth about Fairfield, while the low-life Bruce Kozumplick had now made it to the top. I ground my teeth together for hours, doing plenty of driving in the company van as I ran errands around the area until it was time for lunch. I came in and announced to Bart that I would go home for lunch today – it seemed to make sense.

I got into my faithful Dodge pickup, which I had owned since the first year of college ten years ago, and sped off. The aged truck was refitted with a CD player, allowing me to listen to the Beatles' #1 hit songs, as I usually did. The bag of cookies I kept on the seat was a comfort to me on the drive home. Lunchtime was the only time I could stand to be at home, ever since my father, Bill, moved back in. Well, he didn't really move back in, but he was home so often that I just wanted to be somewhere else.

I took the short drive from the shop down Middlefield to Sterling Avenue, south five miles to Covington, then on to Springer Road until I reached home. We lived in a nice part of town. In Silicon Valley you can tell the best places by the lack of sidewalks. It reminds people of the old days before things got so crowded. The place used to be full of fruit orchards and dirt roads, with no sidewalks.

Dad's car was not in the driveway, so I pulled on in.

Mom was in the tiny living room watching TV, sitting in her little yellow chair on the deep, forest-green shag rug. "Hi Mom, how are you doing?" I said. "Oh Stan, you are home for lunch!" This was very exciting for her. "Sure, why not. It's been a tough day at work."

She quickly disappeared into the kitchen where I found her with the door to the Kenmore open, looking for some cheese and ham for a sandwich. "Would you like mustard?" "Extra," I said, and sat down at the kitchen table.

She brought the sandwich to the table on a plate, and a jar of mustard with a knife. As I spread the mustard on the bread, she brought over a small tray of pastries. "My friends the police officers were here this morning. They stayed for coffee and donuts. These are what's left over." What were on the tray were works of art, not just donuts - the product of one of her old Scandinavian recipes and hours of preparation.

The kitchen had just enough room for the refrigerator, table and four chairs. It was so tight that when two people were seated at the table, many of the cupboards could not be opened without someone having to get out of their chair and stand up. The old linoleum floors were tired and worn, and I remember that my father had told her he was going to replace them at least ten years ago, during one of the few times he was sober for a while. He always went out and got drunk before he could follow through on any promises. I also wondered how he ever did anything sober because he was so incredibly obese.

I looked up at my mom, and the thoughts about my father disappeared. "Tell me what is going on at work today," she said. "Oh, well, it's not really work, it's just that the SOB Bruce Kozumplick has been promoted to deputy laboratory director and was on TV with the President this morning." There was silence. "Oh yes, I remember. Bruce is the oldest of the four boys who used to live next door. How is Midge?" I told her, "Midge is very happy with Bruce." "I bet she is," said

Mom. "It is so wonderful to see your kids grow up to be something." Silence again. What was she saying? Was she also really proud of Bruce? Was I really a "nobody?"

"I used to be somebody until Bruce took it all away!" I huffed, in case she did not remember. "Oh, yes, I remember that you were not too happy with him." She went on, "When he was a little boy he used to pick on the other kids and bully them. I don't think too many people liked him." I listened to this and boiled inside, thinking, "Until high school, when he had every girl in the place coming after him." But I did not verbalize that thought with my mother, who would not understand.

The sandwich was delicious as always, and I rinsed it down with chocolate milk, as usual. "You're not often home for dinner," she said. "Well, you know I am not too fond of having Bill here," referring to my dad. "I have been going out for pizza."

"Your father is doing really well now," she said. "How many weeks dry this time?" I asked. "Only 8 weeks, but I'm not just talking about the amount of time. He really seems different. It seems he has found some really good friends in AA. He found some other men he can really talk to." I wondered what the hell it was they talked about. Then I thought about my ex-girlfriend Karen and how she was in AA. "Do they talk about how crazy the AA women are?" I had a little snicker at that one.

Mom let out a little sigh of exasperation. "He's going to be re-doing the linoleum floor here really soon." I let out a howl of laughter. "I have been listening to that for ten years!" She let out another sigh.

"Will you see Sean this weekend?" she asked me. Karen and I had made our son Sean back when we were students in Berkeley. She got pregnant and left town, and I had not heard from her until about a year ago. "Oh yes," I said. "Let me see, today is Wednesday and I get Sean on Friday night, then I return him on Saturday at noon." "You love seeing him," she said. I did not know what to say at that moment. Of course, it was true.

I just sat there for a moment. It was already 1:15 and my doctor's appointment was at 2:00. I picked up my cell phone and texted the shop that I would be out until 3:30. Just then, I realized that I owed Karen a child-support payment today and I did not have enough money to cover it.

"Mom, I was wondering something." She looked at me. "Do you have some money for me to pay Karen with? I need about a hundred bucks." She said, "That is no problem. Let me look in my purse." Then she left for her bedroom.

I sat in the kitchen alone for a few minutes, listening to the wall clock tick away. I had a flash of terror. I had to see the bitch tonight.

When my mom returned to the kitchen, I was already standing up and had put the dirty dishes into the sink. "I have a doctor's appointment at 2:00." "Oh that's right, you were going to see a psychologist, weren't you?"

"Oh, yes," I said. I took the hundred bucks out of her hand and went out the door. As I was leaving, she called after me, "I love you, Stan." I was too upset from thinking about having to see Karen and how late I was for the doctor's appointment to reply. So I just walked out to the Dodge in the driveway.

There was very little traffic at that time of the day in Mountain View. I drove along Covington to Grant Road. One mile down and on the left was Dr. Sullivan's office. This was my first visit there in quite a while. He had been my mom's shrink when she lost her other son to a car accident about 16 years ago. We had visited one or two times as a family, so I was very familiar with the route.

"Dr. Sullivan will be with you in a moment." I took a seat on the white couch in the waiting room.

I looked around and saw that National Geographic was the only thing worth looking at on the white table in front of the couch. I wished I had brought something to pass the time. There was a "painting" on the wall. A Van Gogh - the sunflowers - like we used to have in the living room when I was a kid. The room had yellow walls and a white carpet. The ticking of the clock was so loud I wondered if it was intentional. Was he trying to drive me crazy? I forced myself to look at the pictures of the slums in the Java story.

I half-wondered why I was seeing a psychiatrist, when I was not even depressed. I was just bewildered, and I wanted some answers. How could I be in a job making just over minimum wage, a job that any high school student could do? Yet I had spent all that time in college and graduate school.

He took me into his office. It was not like a regular doctor's office where you can smell the various doctor smells like rubbing alcohol, detergent, and whatever. It just was like a regular office with books on the shelves. *Psychology of Schizophrenia* was one title; *Physicians Reference* another. Another shelf contained a set of National Geographic issues, probably five years' worth. Apparently, the subscription was a tax write-off.

Dr. Sullivan sat in an office chair at his desk. There was a blue couch, where I was obviously supposed to sit, right across from the desk. It seemed imperative to let him know that I was not crazy. I was just there because I wanted some answers, and I wanted to get right to the point.

"I need for you to explain to me why I would throw away my entire career just to blow the whistle on someone. I was warned that it would ruin me, but I went ahead and did it anyway." I expected him to be interested in what I was saying. Whistleblowers are what Hollywood movies are made of, after all. I thought he would be honored to meet a real whistleblower.

"I see you are here without insurance; have you lost your job?" All he cares about is getting paid, I thought.

"I work in a machine shop. There is no insurance there. My mother is going to pay for the visits."

"What kind of machine shop?"

I felt myself getting a bit angry. "The kind with machines."

"Okay," said the doctor, "I take it you are not here about your current employer." We were beginning to communicate.

"Yes, that's right," I said.

"What medications are you using?" I wondered if he was going to tell me to take some pills and call him later.

"None."

"Are you feeling depressed, or feeling anxiety, or are you thinking about harming yourself?" he asked in rapid order. I said no. The doctor must be required to ask these questions as part of some sort of legal something-or-other. I told myself that it was not his fault that he had to bother with this stuff. It was some lawyer's fault.

"Dr. Sullivan, I am here to ask you a psychology question. I became a whistleblower at Fairfield National Laboratory and as a result, I destroyed my career. Why would anyone do that?"

"There may be many reasons why. But I cannot tell you anything unless you tell me what happened first. So, from the beginning: what are you talking about?"

"I was a witness to crimes committed by a former friend of mine. He was like a brother, but not really"

I tried my best to tell the story in the short period of time that I was there. I stared at the clock the whole time to pace myself, but I still ran out of time. He had to stop me at five of three. Then he said with a smile, "We will schedule another appointment for you," and let me out into the waiting area to see the receptionist.

He held the door open to his office and stood there and said, "I remember your mother; she was a very nice lady." He smiled, but I did not. I scheduled the next appointment for two weeks later at the same day and time.

It was time to get back to the shop. I didn't put the Beatles on because I wanted to do some thinking. There were more cars on the road, I assumed, because of the after-school traffic. That made me think about how Sean would be in school within a year or two. I hadn't even gotten to mention Karen when I was at the doctor because there was so much to talk about. After I explain to the doctor all about her, he will have to answer my next question: why did I ever have anything to do with her? Grant Road goes right to Middlefield Road, which I could just take up to the shop.

Inside the shop, things seemed pretty good on the production floor. All four matic machines were being calibrated for the next job: another lucrative contract from Lockheed. One of the four machines was being used to test and verify the program that runs the machine during the job. It took five people, so everyone was busy, including Bart, Curt and Rudy. It was getting a little warm in the shop, so the front and back doors were open and the fans were running.

"Hey guys!" I announced as I walked up to them. "Stan, we need you here right away," said Bart. It felt good to be needed for something. "We have a delivery that is due by the end of the day," he said, pointing to the finished parts we had made earlier. "Also we need another twenty meters of 20 by 50 6016. They have it ready at Kaiser Metals now." He was referring to a common aluminum alloy ingot with a rectangular cross section of 20 millimeters by 50 millimeters. "We plan on starting this next run tomorrow morning at eight o'clock, so get at it." He chuckled. "Isn't it great when business is doing well?" I said yes, and started to get the keys to the van and my gloves and clipboard together. I was going to pull the van into the back of the shop to load the finished parts. "I already put the parts in the van," said Bart. "Now come into the office to get the money for Kaiser Metals."

This was normal for the shop. They would withdraw cash from the safe to pay for raw materials, because Bart thought that it would give them first priority with suppliers in case there was some sort of supply-chain difficulty. It also made things more fun for me, because I got to carry around large parcels full of cash. My parcel was a zippered Kevlar pouch with a sturdy, cylinder-type lock. I think it cost almost $500 just for the empty pouch. The amount of money we typically transferred within the pouch was often much more than that.

Bart and I went into the office near the safe, and Rudy followed in to get some coffee. Bart spun the dial several times back and forth, then swung the heavy door open. I peeked my head around as I always do, just to catch a look at all that money. The inside of the safe was probably around two cubic feet in volume, and it was half filled with neatly stacked hundred-dollar bills. It always gave me a rush to look at that mountain of money, and I could not help but smile. Rudy was looking in at it too. I looked up at him, but he had a bad expression on his face and quickly turned his head and walked away.

After securing the cash, we locked the safe, and I locked my pouch. The van had a pistol in it, stored in a hidden compartment with a combination lock. I headed out.

The trip went smoothly, especially considering the heavy traffic up U.S. Highway 101 during the late afternoons. My first stop was at the receiving building for Varian Corporation in Redwood City, where I dropped off the completed parts. The second stop was at Kaiser Metals, also in Redwood City, where I picked up the new aluminum ingots. The folks there at Kaiser always chuckle when we come in with that pouch. I think we are the only ones who pay cash.

Because we had reached the end of the day, I arranged it with Bart so that I could just go and do my errand with Karen before returning to the shop with the van. I drove into Palo Alto, down University Avenue, left on Lincoln, then left on Hamilton.

Karen lives in a nice, two-bedroom house. This little road, a few blocks from where Steven Jobs had called home, was one of the places that had made Palo Alto real estate famous throughout the country. Her place was thirteen hundred square feet. Its original sale price in 1955 was $29,000. Two bedrooms, two baths. She paid $1.44 million dollars for it – or should I say the bank paid that much, and the bank still owns it. She could easily afford the payments on her six-figure chemical engineer salary. And I was there to make a child support payment, which I had to borrow from my mom.

I told myself, going up the walkway, that I would not call her any names this time. I would be civilized. Dr. Sullivan was on my side now. I am getting better, I told myself.

She opened the door and cried, "The money!" The irony of the situation gave her intense pleasure. We had met in school, and we made the baby while getting drunk together. Even though she left town while pregnant, she claimed it was my fault all along because I was "abusive." The truth is that this witch (with an IQ of 200) had totally beaten me in the courts, so now I was the slave and she was the master. She had won.

I pulled out my wallet and handed her the five twenties. A big smile blossomed on her face as she grabbed them. She loved feeling victorious. "You can come by and get Sean on Friday at six," she said. "Can I see him now?" I asked. "No," she said. "Why not?" "Because I say so," she said. "Goodbye." She closed the door.

At least the van had a radio in it. I drove down Middlefield Road and traffic was not too bad. I could make the entire eighteen-mile drive to the shop in Mountain View in about 30 minutes that way. Bart and Curt, my lifelong friends, were kind to me and they would pay me time-and-a-half overtime for any time worked after 6 PM. That includes the drive home for that last half hour, even though I had taken time off during the same day. My pay for the last leg of the trip would then be $6.75.

I dropped the van off at the shop, leaving the new metal in the back of it. I got into my Dodge truck, and drove south on Rengstorff Avenue, towards my mom's house. How could there possibly be a worse person in the world than Karen? Oh wait, that would be Bruce. At that point, I realized I was heading towards where my dad was probably hanging out. There was a three-way race to be the worst person in the world. Bruce was in first place and Karen in second. My dad Bill was in third.

Further thoughts on the way home: "Life cannot possibly get worse than this," followed by "How could life be worse than this?" I would soon find out.

Thursday, Day 2

I drove into the shop the next day, at 7:00 AM as always, and I opened the rolling door just like any other time. Arriving early, of course, usually gave me some time to enjoy some donuts and coffee for a few minutes. Today would be different, however.

I looked around and saw that the back window was broken. I walked over to the smashed glass on the floor. The bars over the opening had also been cut. I quickly began to panic. I walked into the office and the file cabinets were open. It appeared that some of the tools were missing. The light was on.

In the corner, to my amazement, the large company safe was on its side. There were some serious dents and scrapes near the hinges and a crowbar on the floor.

I wondered what else had happened. The door lock on the office itself had been broken. The chair was pushed aside. A half-inch power drill and hole saw were also lying on the floor.

I immediately called Bart via the speed dial on my cell phone. "Bart, the shop has been broken into. Get here right away." "What did they get?" "I really don't know." Then Bart said, "Do not wait. Call 9-1-1 now!" and he hung up.

The police operator wanted to know if this was an emergency. "I just discovered a break-in." "Is everyone safe?" "Yes" "Then call the business office at 615-903-6344 when it opens at 8:00 AM."

That half hour was a long wait, and Bart had arrived by then. I started to sweep up the broken glass. I was thinking, correctly as it turned out, that the police did not care about fingerprints. But I decided not to touch the safe, or the tools on the ground near the safe.

Midge arrived just after Bart. "Do you want some coffee?" she asked as she entered: she had a large carafe like every other day and a set of paper cups. "Midge, there was a break-in." She put the coffee aside, silently walking around the shop. "God, God, God!" "Where were Bart and Curt last night?" "Curt went out of town, I think to Anaheim, and Bart went over to Ginger's house."

There was silence.

Then she said, "Bart and Curt both knew they had to be here, what with the crime situation the way that it is." Bart came in and immediately ran into the office. When he ran, his belly bounced up and down a few inches. And when he got into the office, he went right to the file cabinet. "The credit cards are gone. We have to call and cancel them."

He went over to the safe. "They could have cut the thing right open if they could have gotten it over to the milling machine. There is at least fifty thousand dollars in there." There was hardly anything more to do until the police arrived. I walked over and got some of Midge's coffee. Bart had a donut.

We sat and simply tried to figure out who had done this and why. "Mexicans, the stupid Mexicans. You can just tell by the way they walk up and down the street all day long, pretending to look for work," said Bart.

"They keep their little signs out that say 'Looking for Work' when really they are scoping the place out."

I was glad there was some aspirin available, because my head was hurting.

Bart had recently gone through some changes, now that Ginger was in his life. It seemed he was over at her place at least half the time. She seemed okay, not nearly as bad as Karen. Bart thought that she was something really special. Ginger was the only girlfriend that Bart had ever had, I think. Bart had made a lot of money running this shop over these last years with his brother Curt, probably over half a million in profit per year, after paying all the machinists.

Bart and Curt had paid off the mortgage on Midge's house and bought her a new Cadillac. They also paid off their dad's mortgage just because they could.

Inside the office, we moved past the "discovery" that the intruders were Mexican to amazement that they had known the place would be empty last night. Of course, usually either Bart or Curt or both of them would have been there.

Bart said, "Maybe they were watching us close up shop at the end of the day yesterday." "Yes," Midge chimed in. "There was a car parked across the street at five o'clock last night and the night before. There was a Mexican-looking guy just sitting out there."

The machinists, Josh and Seth, arrived at eight as usual. Bart told them to just go ahead like it was a normal day. "Did you guys notice anyone casing the place out last night?" They both said no. Rudy showed up next, all shabby as usual, with his hair tied in a ponytail. He knew that it was not a good idea to keep his hair long while working with these machines, because a little entanglement with the spinning machine could quickly lead to an on-the-job fatality. But he thought that the ponytail was just cool, and girls had always seemed to like whatever he did.

He went over to the machine he'd been working on the night before and immediately started programming it. "I'm behind," he said without a smile. That seemed a little strange to me.

The day proceeded as normal after the cops left at about 9:30. They just had a few questions and were not concerned with anything beyond filling out a report. The report, I supposed, is provided to the victims so they can file an insurance claim. This situation, as far as the cops were concerned, was just business-as-usual. They assigned a junior member to dust the safe and the tools for fingerprints, but I don't remember hearing that there would be any follow-up report.

Well, look at this, I thought: the cops do nothing, do not give a damn, and collect a paycheck bigger than mine. I stood there watching this happen, feeling confident my IQ was probably seven times higher than the sum of all of theirs. I had lost everything, job-wise, but only because I had decided to blow the whistle on the game that Bruce Kozumplick was playing at Fairfield.

Bruce makes so much money at Fairfield that he could easily have paid off both Midge's and George's mortgages in just a year or two. But he would never lift a finger for anyone. The younger kids had paid them off doing real work. As I stood there looking at the cops, I became extremely mad as my thoughts whirled around Bruce.

As I said, it was a regular day for Seth and Josh. They put in a full day each. Rudy left early, probably around 2 PM, because, he said, he had to meet with Brendalyn and make up again.

After Seth and Josh were gone, Midge, Bart, and I had a sit-down over some pizza. Bart was drinking a beer. He offered me one as he always did. I always said no and always felt myself getting angry. Midge said that we would be allowed to shoot them "as long as their dead bodies were inside the property. That is the way it is, at least in Texas." She and her family had been there for generations, all the way up until the 1970s.

There was no further discussion about the legal details. We began formulating a plan. Bart had the first say. "There is something I want to show you, Stan." He went over to a steel cabinet that had a large padlock across the front. Opening it up, he pulled out something that looked like an ordinary hunting rifle, except that it did not have a stock. "It is a 50 cal." "Bart!" Midge said. He had an ammunition container out on the table and the gun beside it. A second trip to the cabinet and he got a tripod. "The tripod is required for this caliber of weapon." The tripod was spread apart and the gun mounted on top of it. The trigger was electronic and the sight was a laser pointer. A third trip to the metal cabinet produced a small box with a nine-inch TV screen. It was a camera and a remote control. "The spotting laser points at the target, which you view with the camera. Then you push the button, it goes kaboom, and the target is dead." The ammunition for this weapon consisted of huge bullets; probably ten times the size of any I had seen before.

I picked one up. "Holy shit." "Watch your tongue," said Midge. One of those two words or their combination was against God's way or her religion, or whatever. I apologized to her, but that was just to be nice.

The sun was down by about eight o'clock so in the intervening hours, we set up the rig so most of the entryway to the shop would be covered. The lights were lowered down by about 8:30 and we had the infrared lenses in place. The combination of night goggles with low levels of illumination in the shop made the trap an effective one. It seemed like it would work perfectly.

"Now let's get that Mexican," said Bart. After closing the shop and turning out the lights, he got in his Chevy pickup and I got in my old Dodge and we both drove away. I drove south on Middlefield Avenue and he drove north. We each drove a few blocks down and parked off on side streets. Bart crept slowly back to the shop under the shadows, as did I. He entered through the back door, keeping the inside lights low. He was ready to drink Yuban coffee all night, and so was I.

There was an abandoned Ford Focus in the parking lot next door, so I sat inside it, kept a low profile and waited, cell phone in my lap, and a large coffee on the floor. My role was to act as lookout: the one who would wait and warn Bart, via text message, when the Mexican arrived. Despite all the coffee, after an hour I was already thinking about sleep.

A couple of people walked by, but I kept cool and they did not see me. The Focus was parked probably 60 feet away from the sidewalk in some shadows, and I could see the spot at the shop where the break-in had happened the night before.

It seemed like days went by, but it was only a few hours. There was no foot traffic anymore and I got quite sleepy, but it was no time to sleep.

I called Curt in Anaheim and informed him of the situation and the status of the stakeout. He was staying down south that night and would not return until noon the next day. The conversation ended, and I snuck out of the car to pee and to refill my coffee at the 7-11.

I walked past the guy behind the counter, who was probably 200 pounds overweight. It was an outrage to even have to look at him. His nametag said "Bud" and he tried some sort of joke about needing coffee this time of the night. I gave him two bucks and stood there, chugging the coffee down. I wore a polite veneer over my disgust. Ice cubes in the coffee helped me to chug it down faster. I did not have any more room left after the two large cups.

After getting back to the Focus, I had an idea. It had been years since I had partied with Ross, my old friend from the pizza parlor. Rudy, Ross, Steve and I used to drink pitchers of beer together. Because I had quit drinking a couple of years ago, I had not seen too much of Ross. But he was one guy who had been around the block a few times, and knew the right people to get the right supplies.

Friday, Day 3

M y pickup truck was only a block away and it was still only midnight. I texted Bart: "at 7-11 bak soon." Then I started to walk down the dark back street. There was a text reply "get bak now," but I was headed out, ignoring him.

"What ever happened to the old days," I thought. The two of us, along with Curt, used to drive down into the Los Padres National Forest and hunt squirrels together with our .22 rifles. We must have killed a thousand per trip, and we must have made a thousand trips in Midge's old Cadillac. After each squirrel death, we laughed. Towards the end, I remember we were switching to larger-caliber rifles for a surer kill. Curt used a 223 varmint rifle, and then Bart got a .30-30 carbine. I had to outdo the others and got a .30-06 deer rifle that would literally cut the squirrel in two.

Bart was as serious as a funeral about the business lately. The break-ins over the last year seemed to preoccupy him. He was using a weapon system that probably could not be justified based on cost vs. benefit analysis, but it was a good tax write-off.

He perched in the rafters of the shop and had the Russian-made night goggles and a clean view of the spot where the break-in had happened the night before.

The entire shop had been wired with electronic alarms by his uncle, Milt, but no one knew that one of the windows in the shop had not been properly wired for the alarm. That was the place the break-in had happened. Was it Uncle Milt who had broken in? Who else? But he was the one who had originally loaned Bart and Curt the money to get the shop started. He is someone who is "rolling in money," so to speak. But there was no one else who even knew about the hole in the security, not even Josh or Seth. The people who knew were Bart, Curt, myself, Rudy and Midge.

The Dodge was faithful as always, starting promptly. I texted Bart, "wait a minute." I headed out of that area of town, towards Ross' house.

"Hey Stan Hall, long time no see," said Ross when he opened the door. A huge waft of dope smoke came out, more fragrant than a bottle of perfume. What a smell. I walked in and the bong was centrally placed on the dining room table. "Hey Ross, I see you are now in the medicine business," referring to the medical marijuana law passed in the state. There was a scale on the table next to the bong and an entire overflowing salad bowl of the exotic material.

I went right for the couch. He offered me a malt liquor. NO. How about some wine? There was a gallon jug sitting on the coffee table. What was he thinking? I guess he did not know that I had quit drinking. "Ross, I don't drink anymore." There was a stunned look of disbelief for just a moment, and then he winced. "You don't? How did you do that?"

I told him that I had just had enough of it. I told him about how I had started driving in blackouts and could have ended up killing a half a dozen people, including myself. Then I told him about the night when I had crossed over the Dumbarton Bridge in a blackout and arrived at my mom's house without knowing how I got there.

"By the way, how is your mom?" he asked, changing the subject. His eyes were glazed over, as I remembered they always had been. He had probably been smoking a lot of dope. "Mom is good. She lives by herself back on old Springer Road just like before. She and Dad are getting along. Sometimes I see him there. "They must be getting old now?" he asked. "Yes, I think 55 is pretty old, all right." "Both my parents were dead before they turned 55," said Ross.

"Ross, what I want to know is whether you have any white crosses." "White crosses? You want those? Yeah, I have a few." I explained about the break-in at the shop and how Bart and I were watching the place all night long. "Let me see."

White crosses are the nickname for amphetamine pills, which were commonly used by doctors and nurses years ago to help them do long shifts at the hospitals where they were working. I first heard about them from my mom, an ex-nurse, who said they really helped sometimes. I knew that Ross had used them. For instance, there was that night that he, Rudy and I had closed down the pizza parlor and driven all the way to Santa Cruz and consumed a keg of beer on the beach. He had enough white crosses for all three of us.

We went into the back room, technically his bedroom, and waded through all the trash to the closet in the back. There were piles of clothes and bed sheets that needed washing. Back in the corner of the room was a hamster in a cage. He pointed at the thing,

"That's Henry. He is stoned right now." I looked in the food bowl and there was a half-eaten chunk of marijuana.

Ross came out of the closet. "This is all I have." He opened his hand and there were seven pills there, two white ones and five brown ones. "Great!" I said. "Do you have a glass of water?" "In the kitchen."

I remember walking out of the bedroom and across the living room floor, thinking about how great it was to have a friend like Ross. There were no clean glasses in the kitchen, so I put all the pills in my mouth and put my head under the faucet, filled my mouth with water and swallowed. He watched me do this and said, "WAIT! You are not taking all of those now are you?" Most certainly. I had, already.

"Dude, you've got to take it easy with those." I listened to him, all the while thinking that he was just a stoner. "What are you talking about?" "Those white pills were white crosses, but those brown ones were Adderall." "Adderall? What's that?" "Adderall, have you heard of it?" "No," I said. Ross said, "I stopped using it because it was making me whacky, and I was hardly using any of it."

Then he went into a story about what had happened the last time he had used the stuff. He was with his friend Jonathan and they had a dozen of the pills. Ross had put one in his mouth and opened the other one up and sprinkled it on the marijuana in his dope pipe. He said as soon as he had smoked the pipe-load, a whole bunch of spiders had come out of the television set. They came right at him. He started screaming and ran out the front door of the house. Then the spiders chased him down the sidewalk and they seemed to keep up with him no matter how fast he ran. A car almost hit him before he realized what was going on.

The message that I heard was to never smoke anything, no matter what; but especially marijuana mixed with Adderall. Damn, that marijuana is no good stuff, I thought. I have never liked it and it has made Ross into such a lazy guy. I didn't want to tell him that I had such negative thoughts about his dope smoking because he had been such a good friend to me for so long. The combination of MJ and Adderall must be extremely lethal, I thought.

We sat back down on the couch and he turned on the radio. Some sort of oldies channel was playing a Beatles songfest. We talked about the good old days while Ross had a couple of bong hits and a glass of wine. We talked about Steve and whatever he might be into now in prison. "Do you think Steve is out yet?" I asked. "It has only been five years," he said. "Steve was one weird dude. He just loved talking about the Persian Gulf War. It was like he never left that place."

My fingers were tingling; "Helter Skelter" was playing. My ears were ringing. The song sounded strange, like a kind of music I had never heard before.

"You remember the Manson Family?" he said. I faintly recalled. "The Manson family was listening to this song when they were on LSD so they went on a rampage, killing Sharon Tate and the La Bianca family." "They did?" Ross went into the outer room and returned with a book. "Here is the uncensored version of what they did." He opened the book and inside there were photographs of Sharon Tate, apparently taken by the police, with her entire abdomen ripped open and her guts spilled on the ground. I could see from the photograph on the adjacent page that she had been a beautiful blonde, but they had gouged both her eyes out and cut out her unborn child.

I looked at the black-and-white photos and got a little queasy. This had to be the sickest thing I had ever seen. My fingers were starting to tingle as the white crosses and the Adderall started to kick in. "Ross, don't you have any color photos?" I said with a straight face. He roared with laughter and spilled his wine down his arm. "DUDE! You will never change!" I was laughing really hard as well (and not looking at the photos anymore). I got another funny line. "Ross, abortion wasn't even legal back then." "Sick, sick, sick" he said.

The substances were entering my system, waking me up significantly. So what, I thought, I wont get to sleep until noon. "Awesome Ross!! You are a friend among friends!! Wish I could stay and have a drink with you but I don't drink any more. I told you that already, didn't I?" We both laughed. "Drinking is no good for you," he said.

I walked out the door, making the expected remark that he and I should get together again some time. I did not know at that point that I would be returning within an hour. I suspected he wanted me to start drinking so it would be like old times. I would never do that. I turned around: "Ross do I owe you anything for those pills?" "Nope" he said.

I took off in the Dodge and headed back towards the shop. Wow, I had to find that oldies channel on my radio. KKSP, all oldies, all the time - Beatles special. "While My Guitar Gently Weeps." That guy George can play. Hell yes, I hope they play "For the Benefit of Mr. Kite" and the best song they'd ever made: "I Am the Walrus."

It was so great to be back at the shop with old Bart. I drove up to the front and knocked on the door. "Hey Bart! Did you shoot any Mexicans yet?" Damn I was funny. He flew out the door after a few seconds. "Shut up," he whispered angrily. "Come inside." Bart was not cool to the excitement of the evening. "Bart, I really want to help. Really. I really want to help. Really, Really." He was annoyed. "Your truck should not be parked in front. You are supposed to hide out in that Focus. Shut up and stay low."

Obediently, I went to the Dodge and drove it to the back of the 7-11. This was an all-night 7-11, so I had gotten lucky. Bought some chocolate brownies. Some Diet Coke. Oh my God, this is so great. Okay so I had gained a few pounds lately, under the stress that my ex-girlfriend, Karen, had put me under. She knows how much I like to see our son Sean, and she won't let me see him more than one day every two weeks.

I sat back in the cab of the Dodge with a package of cookies. God was I hungry. They were gone. Thirsty. The Diet Coke was kind of taking care of that. I got out again and got some Fig Newtons. Texted Bart "Lunch Break." No reply. The oldies channel was playing "Lady Madonna" and it was incredible. I could not help myself; I got out of the cab, wandered into the parking lot and just danced to the music!

Damn, the time had flown by – I texted Bart again: "Lunch break over." No reply.

The Dodge stayed at the back of the 7-11, and I crossed over Middlefield Avenue to the darker side of the street and made my way along in the shadows towards the shop. At about Baylands Avenue, I turned a left corner into the district where the shop was, and saw flashing red lights. There must have been six cop cars in front.

I walked through the alleyway near the shop and came in around the back. One cop was there, blocking my path. I pretended to turn around but dove behind an abandoned Toyota Corolla and circled back. As she walked past, I came around the back of the car past her and into the entryway of the shop. Four cops were standing there with Bart – and Bart did not look very comfortable. He was gesturing and trying to make some sort of point, I was not sure what.

Near the place where the break-in had happened the night before was a pool of blood and a body covered in a jacket. The body was spread over a wide area of the floor. I walked closer to it – the person had been literally cut in two by the rifle shot. Someone had put a plastic garbage bag over the top half of the body. There was hair, bound into a ponytail, sticking out of the side of the garbage bag. It was Rudy.

As my body absorbed the substances inside me and my eyes absorbed the sight before me, I started screaming. The cops and Bart all looked at me but it was too much for me to just stand there and have them stare at me. I ran out the door and just kept running. I ran past the Focus, and all the way down to Middlefield Road, down to the 7-11. The cop sirens were on. I got in my Dodge and drove the back way to Ross's house and ran inside.

Ross was asleep on the couch. "Ross, you have to help me hide my truck. I have to put it in your garage." "Why?" "The cops are after me!"

"What for?" "I'll explain later. Where is the door opener?" Ross pointed to an opener on the wall in the kitchen and I pushed the button. I ran out to the Dodge, drove it quickly in and hit the button again, all the time hearing the cop sirens whistling away.

I ran up to Ross and just started to cry. I was so weak from the running and seeing Rudy dead. "You can't let them find me! Ross! They can't find me!!"

"Why not?" I explained the situation. Rudy was dead. Ross knew Rudy and he knew that Rudy had been my friend since middle school. "Shit!" Ross said. "Shit is an understatement," he continued. "I have been doing a lot of selling to Rudy lately." "What?" I said. "Rudy is into cocaine and crack. He has also been playing stud poker and losing his ass off."

We were still using present tense, as though he were still alive. "Oh my God. . . ." There was silence for quite some time. I sat on the couch. There was wine right in front of me but I would not drink it. We both looked at each other. "We are screwed." Ross and I just sat there for another two hours, until it was about 7:30 AM and the morning traffic was starting up. My cell phone had a text message. It was from the police and it said that I should come to the station to answer some questions.

Ross and I started speaking and then my phone rang. It said the Mountain View Police were calling. I ignored it. "Stan, you cannot let them know about me." Just tell them that you don't know why Rudy was breaking in." We talked more. My arms were shaking and my voice was shaking. "Calm down; you did not commit any felony," he said, "maybe a misdemeanor." I was not too sure. How about conspiracy to commit murder? No, that wasn't what it was. The phone rang again. Police again. Ignore again.

I went out into the Dodge and opened up the garage, wished Ross well and sped away. When I had gotten about five blocks down the road, I called the cops back. Answering the phone was a woman's voice, "Hello, this is Debbie O'Connor!" It was the blonde haired lady cop. "This is Stan Hall." She said, "Yes I know. You lost your friend today and you are very scared. We just want to talk to you. Please just go to the machine shop." I followed her suggestion and that was where I went.

When I pulled into the driveway, all their faces turned to look at me. I thought the handcuffs would come out, but they did not. "Sorry for the loss of your friend, but we have some questions for you," the lady officer, Debbie O'Connor, said. Her Irish name was clearly spelled out on her white nametag on her blue suit. I thought she must have had an Irish cop for a dad and wanted to be like him. Midge was there next to me. Bart was in one of the police cars in the back seat, probably in trouble.

Officer O'Conner said, "This is Officer Neal Randles, who needs to ask you some questions." Officer Randles was a man of probably 35, with thin hair and a very serious look on his face. "Stan, I understand you have some knowledge about the homicide." I swallowed hard. "Homicide?" I thought to myself. Then I looked in his eyes. "No. I don't know what you are talking about." "You are an employee here?" "Yes." I looked at Midge. "Did you participate in a plan to kill an intruder last night?" I knew that I did not have to answer that question. "I will not answer that question," I said to his face. "Were you here last night after the shop closed?" "Yes NO!" I said. "I do not have to answer that question either." "Why not?" said the officer. "Self-incrimination." He smiled and said, "Okay," in a soft voice. "You are under arrest for the murder of Rudy Goodman." He took my wrists behind my back and put on handcuffs. He marched me to the same cop car where Bart was, and put me in the back seat with him. He smiled a warm smile. "You two are going downtown."

Midge was crying. And she went up to the side of the car and started yelling at Neal Randles. "How could you do this? This happened inside the shop on our private property!" She screamed. Officer Randles turned to her and said, "How do you think Rudy's mom feels about that?" Midge was screaming, "Rudy was a no-good lazy SOB and worthless scum of the Earth!" Officer Randles said, "Mrs. Kozumplick, what did you say? Did you say you were in on the planning of this crime?" He turned to his nearby cop buddy and said, "I think this is a conspiracy to commit murder!" With that, the officer grabbed Midge's wrists and put on another pair of handcuffs. Midge just barely fit in the seat next to Bart and me. The three of us were sped away to the police station.

I had to pee so badly that I can hardly believe I made it all the way there. The three of us knew better than to say anything to each other while in the car. When we arrived, Midge was let out first, and greeted by a lady cop for further processing. We waited in the car for what seemed like an hour. Then both Bart and I were led out, the handcuffs removed, and we were placed in a cell with about a dozen other men, mostly smelly drunks. God did I have to pee. I made may way over to the toilet and got in line behind two smelly black men, and after what seemed like another hour, finally got my turn to pee. My head was about to explode, as well.

After a few more hours, Bart and I were led out of the cell into a small room where Officer Randles was waiting. He said, "Now will be your chance to come clean on your stories about what happened. Your stories must agree with one another or you shall both remain here in custody until you decide to tell the truth. I will be speaking with Bart first, and then you, Stan. An officer named Black took me into the hallway for what seemed like an hour while Officer Randles questioned Bart. Then Officer Black took me in to see Officer Randles while he held Bart in the hallway.

It was the Prisoner's Dilemma for real. This famous dilemma is based on the simple theory that cooperation between the two prisoners gets the best outcome for both. That is, they must both tell the same lies, then they both go free, eventually. If one breaks with the "game" and blames the other prisoner for the crime, the one who breaks out will go free immediately and the other one will end up serving a long sentence. No one can predict the outcome of the game in advance.

"Okay Stan, tell me your story." I replied, firmly, "No." Officer Randles said, "Bart already told me everything: about how you had a break-in and set up a trap that the two of you were watching. You had no idea that it was Rudy who would be breaking in." He had gotten the story one way or another. "We found drugs in Rudy's blood." I said nothing, knowing that they wanted to put Ross and probably Bart away for some charges. "I demand a lawyer." "Goddamn it!" he said, and slammed his left fist down on the table. "Lawyer" I shouted back.

He stood up, stared sideways for a half a minute, and then turned back to me with a devilish smile and said, "I know your mother and I'm going to tell her what you did." Then he let out a howling laugh and said nothing more.

Both Bart and I were put back in the cell with the other prisoners, but the crowd had thinned down somewhat. I had to share a cell with such low-life scum. It got to be six o'clock when Curt finally arrived with a lawyer for Bart, a Mr. McKlusky. Boy, was I glad to see Curt. The lawyer said to Bart that he was free to go – he was out on bail, which was paid by Curt. Midge was also free to go, and he told her that the appearance in court would be in about two weeks.

My lawyer had not arrived. After a while, an officer arrived for Bart and led him away. He wished me well but strangely did not look me in the eye as he departed.

Saturday, Day 4

I slept that night on the concrete floor of the jail cell. More drunks were put in at night and released in the morning. At about 9 AM my mom arrived with our family attorney, Mr. Schultz. Mom was crying. "Stan, how could this have happened? They must have made some sort of mistake." I assured her that they had made a mistake. "Mr. Schultz said that the court has required a drug test on me, and that we may be able to leave by 3 PM if all goes well." My mother was still in tears. She sobbed, "Stan, you are not using dr-dr-drugs?" She could not even get the word out. "No Mom. This is all a mistake." Mr. Schultz warned us not to speak to each other now, because our conversations were being recorded. I told him I knew that. Mom shut up.

The drug test was just a blood draw in a side room, which took about an hour. Mr. Schultz was simply holding my mother's hand at $250 per hour for that period. We stood in front of the magistrate at about 3 PM and I was released without comment. I guess I passed the drug test. The full hearing would be in two weeks.

Mr. Schultz said my truck was in the impound yard, and I could go get it after three days. For now I just had to stay with my mom on Springer Road. He drove us there and let us off. It was an incredible relief to get home. My mom said she was feeling sick and had to lie down for a while.

After about a half hour at home I was bored. It was not time to call the Kosumplicks, however: the cops were probably tapping the phone line. I got so bored that I started thinking about drinking my mom's wine out of the refrigerator. But nothing will get me to drink. Drinking is for losers.

I went into my mom's bedroom at 6 pm. She had certainly been in bed for a while. I asked her if there was any problem. "No, not really. I just got dizzy for a moment and needed to lie down." Above her bed was her favorite Monet. Her poodle was next to her. "Hi Cujo," I said and scratched the thing on the head. She said, "Well, I guess it's time to get up and make dinner." She swung around and put on her shoes, brushed her hair back and went into the bathroom. It was probably about 6:15, and I went out into the living room to catch the evening news. The news show was more interesting than usual, because it contained a segment on the shooting at the machine shop in Mountain View. There was new evidence that had come in. The man who had been killed had cocaine in his bloodstream.

At around 6:45 I noticed that Mom had not come out of the bathroom. I went over and knocked on the door, and heard some strange kind of scratching sound. The door was unlocked, so I pushed it open and it stopped, hitting my mother's head. She was lying on the floor. I continued to push the door open and found that she was not breathing.

I called 911 and they wanted to know the emergency. "My mother was lying on the floor and she is probably dead." "Are you sure?" "Well, pretty sure, her heart is not beating and she is lying on the floor." The ambulance was at our house almost immediately. The poodle was barking furiously as they took my mother away. "Yes, she has passed away," said one of the EMTs.

I sat there alone, silently, in the house. I don't know how much time went by. It was well past dark now. There was no one to call. Mom was dead. I fed the poodle and watched TV. Not even this could make me drink.

I called Karen and told her that my mother had died. "I never liked her," was her reply, which was just about on par for Karen. "How is my boy," I asked. "Your boy? I heard about what you and Bart did at the machine shop. You can forget about seeing Sean again. I have a restraining order on you." "FUCKING BITCH!" I yelled into the phone and slammed it down.

After a few minutes it was too quiet in the house. The only sound besides the TV was the dog's breathing. The despair was beginning to set in. My mom was dead.

I went over to my mom's purse, and her car keys were in there. I got the keys and just drove toward the machine shop. Block after block went by, and then I arrived. It was 9 PM and the place was totally locked up; no one was there. I turned around and went down Fulton, to Middlefield, down Sterling and up to Ross's house. His car was in the driveway.

I walked up to the door and let myself in. Ross came up and said, "What are you doing here? I thought you got busted." "No, they let me go, pending something or other." I sat down in the couch. "My mom died." "WHAT?" he cried. "My mom just died this afternoon. They said it was some kind of aneurysm or something. A stroke or heart attack. She went into the bathroom and just died."

Ross's friend Jonathan was there, sitting on the couch with a bag of pills in his lap. "Hey that's a drag, man. Take some of these." I said no, not now. "What kind of pills are those anyway?" "Pure Adderall – these are 60s." "Cool," I said. "Yes, this stuff will send you to Jupiter." "Well, maybe I could use some. How much do you want for them?" "A buck a pill, or fifteen dollars for twenty." "Okay, I'll take twenty," and I handed him a twenty. He gave me a five back.

He wanted to tell me all about when his mom died; how everyone just freaked out because she had a lot of money and all the kids were fighting over all of it. "That sounds pretty bad," I said, basically just pretending to be interested. My only sibling was my brother who had been gone for 13 years since the car crash. I guessed my mom's house was mine now. But that was little consolation.

Sunday, Day 5

A fter midnight I drove home and tried to get some sleep. At 7 AM there was a knock on the door. I threw on some clothes. Passing a window, I saw that there was a cop car in the driveway. I opened the door and it was Officer O'Connor. Frightened, I stood back. She stood in the doorway and just cried. "I am so, so sorry about your mother," she said. I kept listening. "My EMT friend was here for the call and said it was Mrs. Hall, Stan Hall's mother who had just died. I'm so sorry."

It seemed at the time that she probably just wanted to get me to accidentally spill the beans about how Rudy was hooked on drugs that Ross had sold him, and that the whole ambush had been planned for the purpose of killing the intruder without warning, which is against California law and a felony. I was fairly certain of all this. I just closed the door on her.

That this was all some sort of conspiracy by the police was beginning to occur to me. I really did not know at that point exactly what they were up to, but I was having some sort of clarity.

The poodle and I were getting bored just sitting inside, so we went for a walk. Upon passing the house next door, our neighbors, Sam and Lenore Campbell, came out and asked me how my mother was doing. I told them that she had passed away at about six o'clock the night before. They acted so sad, and wanted to tell me about how my mom used to really love the flowers they had planted in front of their house. But I did not care, so I just walked away with Cujo. The rest of the walk was fairly uneventful – I really did not want anyone to bother me. Cujo and I came around the final corner to my mom's house and the poodle became very excited.

In the driveway was my father's car. Bill Hall was inside the house and I was grumbling profanities to myself. He had already decided that I would go no further, so he met me at the front door. "Give me Cujo – that's my dog." I did not know what to say and I certainly did not want the dog, so I gave it to him. "Here's your dog, fatso," I said.

"How can you call me that at a time like this? When your mother, your mother has just, just . . . " He could not get the words out. "I just lost your mother." He turned around with the poodle and let himself into the house. Before closing the door he said, "You are not welcome here until you straighten out and begin to do the right thing."

"God Almighty, Fat Bill has taken my house," I thought. "That asshole – that fat piece of shit!" I pounded on the door. "Let me in!" But he would not. I went around the side gate and into the side yard, and then into the backyard. As I approached the rear French doors, I could see him sitting in the living room at the table with a beer in his hand. He had started drinking again. The French doors were locked, but there was a brick lying on the ground in front.

I grabbed the brick and smashed it through the glass in the left side door, my arm traveling all the way through the glass up to the elbow. I continued reaching in so as to unlock the door from the inside. Bill had not figured out what was going on yet, and he was unable to make it to the door in time to stop me from getting in. I pulled my arm back through the broken glass, and felt some intense cutting on my skin and warm blood gushing along my arm. Nonetheless I pushed the door open, and pushed it hard, hitting him in the forehead. He rose up and tried to punch me while I was coming in, but I held up the brick and he hit it with his hand, making a loud sound. He screamed in pain. Then I took the brick and hit him squarely in the face, and he stopped screaming and fell to the ground. He fell so that his face was right at my feet, so I began kicking him in the face, over and over again. He made no sound. Blood was gushing out of his nose.

All of a sudden, it occurred to me that this was probably some sort of crime and I should not get caught, even though this was my house and Bill was in here illegally. It was time to go.

Back in Mom's car, a Ford Fusion, I sped down Springer Road towards God-knows-where. My drunk bastard fucking father was just lying there as far as I knew, and I didn't care. The thought occurred to me that I should go to a bar and just drink it all away, but I would not do that. I started thinking about the drunks in the jail cell and how bad they had smelled. What scum.

It seemed to me next that this automobile was going to get me caught by the cops, so I had better just find a place to put it. So I pulled into a Safeway grocery store parking lot and just left it there. Across from the

Safeway is a bus stop, and the bus goes all the way up El Camino almost to San Francisco. What an easy getaway. I got out at a nice transit station in San Mateo and just sat down. Rest and regain. I was sitting on a concrete bench and a woman came up to me and said, "Do you want me to call 911 for your arm?" Looking down, I saw it was quite a mess. I could see why she had asked. Not only was my shirt soaked in blood, but there was also a gash on my thumb that was so huge that it looked like a piece of meat was hanging off.

"No thanks, I'm fine." There was a public water fountain nearby and I used it to wash off. Nothing would stop the bleeding, however. I needed attention, and Ross was the only person that I could go to. It was scary, in a way, because Ross lived only a few blocks from Mom's house. The same bus that took me here could take me all the way back, so I got in line at the bus stop to take the 22 all the way back to Mountain View. After about an hour I was within about six blocks of his house, so I got off. Pressure on the wound had slowed the bleeding down. The meat was still hanging off my thumb.

Back at Ross's house, he was not there. It was the middle of the day in the middle of the week and he is a schoolteacher. He once showed me where he had hidden a key for the house, so I used it to get in. Inside, there were some towels that I cut up to use as bandages for my arm. I could not find any ointment to put on the wounds, so some grease from the kitchen would have to do. No antibiotics of any kind were available. I wrapped up the damaged thumb with a simple rag and then took a workshop glove out of the garage and put it over the bandage.

Now I knew that I would have to the leave the state. I figured that they probably thought it is some sort of crime, beating up my dad, even though I knew better. The SOB deserved it. Now, how do I get away? Ross was out driving in his car and there was nothing to get me anywhere. Maybe he still had that old motorcycle that he used to have. It would be in the corner of the yard, maybe. Yes it was there, yes it was covered with cobwebs, and no it had no gas in the tank. But the lawnmower had gas.

I made up a one-gallon transfer tank to move the gas from the lawnmower to the motorcycle using some garden hose. It seemed to work. No problem, except that the gas really burned when it sprayed onto my chopped-up thumb. The motorcycle started. Even though there was no helmet to be found, I could still travel a long way without one. There is a helmet law but they never enforce it.

When I was just about to leave, I noticed a book on the shelf. *Beyond Good and Evil*. It seemed like just the thing I needed to read about, so I set the book in the saddlebag and took off. I left a thank-you note for Ross and a hundred bucks. I still had plenty of money at this time, having taken all the money out of my mother's purse. I was beginning to develop a short temper for the bullshit that society places on us: calling certain things good and other things evil. It was arbitrary, as far as I was concerned.

This was going to be a long motorcycle trip, so I stopped at the 7-11 to pick up a supply of soda pop. In the parking lot, since I was planning to ride all the way to Mexico, I took all twenty of the brown pills that I had in my pocket. Awesome, I thought.

I was well within the speed limit on Highway 280, headed south on this old Honda bike, when a cop car showed up in my rear view mirror with its lights on, cherry-flasher style. Certainly this was some sort of mistake. I pulled over and the officer approached me, asking for a driver's license. "Officer, what is the matter?" He looked at my driver's license. "Mr. Hall, we have a helmet law in this state." "I don't need a helmet!" I said to him. Things were becoming clear. I have rights. I am good. He is evil. This was the beginning of a new awakening, or so it seemed at the time.

He returned to his car and got on the radio. After a few minutes he came back and said. "We have a warrant for your arrest." "What for?" I said. "You are under arrest for domestic battery." "Bullshit! These are lies!" The officer was just a pawn in a silly game, a game that he could not understand.

He told me to get into the back of his car, after putting a pair of handcuffs on me. "Please, officer, let me have my book – it is very important that I have my book." He went into the saddlebag and got the book and inspected it. He verified that there was nothing hidden inside. "Nietzsche? You read him?" He took the book and kept it in the front of the cop car while I rode in the back.

The idiot cop had mispronounced the name of the great philosopher, Fredrich Wilhelm Nietzsche. He said it like "Ny-Chee," like Cheetos, the things you munch on while watching football on TV. "What a dope," I thought. "Why do we have such idiots wearing badges and carrying guns? Our lives are protected by *them*?" He said, "Who are you talking to?" I did not answer.

He took the book and put it on the seat next to him while I rode in the back, handcuffed. In the cop car, it became more and more clear how this whole system of so-called good and evil is thoroughly corrupt. "Our cops think this is a game, like a football game!" I announced. "Who is going to score the next points? Who is going to throw the long bomb?" "Long bomb?" The cop, Officer Fernandez, was clueless. He thought this was all real. "The 49ers just scored a touchdown!" I shouted out, trying to make him understand how much of a hoax he was involved in.

While he was driving, I could hear that he was speaking in secret code on the police radio. "EPS, EPS case, VMC VMC!" I had to laugh. He was talking on the radio, but he was talking like David Bowie; "Ground Control to Major Tom." I could not stop laughing. He was imitating David Bowie on the police radio.

We went along Highway 280 for about six miles and then just kept going south past the road that would have gone to the cop station. He kept going and I began to scream "What are you doing? What are you doing?" He yelled out, "Shut up you, we are putting you in a motel." I began wondering: "A motel? What the hell?" He took the Bascom Avenue off-ramp, turned left and then went into Valley Medical Center, using the north wing entrance.

"What are they doing?" I wondered.

I was put into a waiting area in the psych unit. A psychiatric unit! All these people are looking at me and speaking in code. Something about Manchurian Candidate. Space Cadet. I was convinced that this was code for Helter Skelter. They are going to cut me open like the Manson Family gutted Sharon Tate.

Instead, I was put in an entryway in front of a computer. The officer was standing next to me while information came up on the screen. "Is this your correct address?" I look and it has my mom's house address. "My mom is dead!" I yelled. They want to torture me by forcing me to look at that. "I hate you!" "Put down that he said that was his address." the cop tells the lady inputting the data.

I looked on the screen and it had everything about me. Birth date. Mother and father. Graduation from high school, college, graduate school in chemical engineering, driver's license, Dodge pickup truck. Diagnosis: Schizophrenia. "What?" I ask her. "It says I'm schizophrenic." She said "The doctor input that diagnosis." I hadn't seen any doctor.

After another hour of waiting with the cop next to me, they took me through some locked metal doors into the psych area. I was admitted into a room where all the staff nurses and other patients could watch me to see if I was schizophrenic. Then they left the door open to my room. So I walked over and closed it. Then someone came by five minutes later and opened it again. People are staring and laughing at me. What did they think is so funny? The bastards.

Monday, Day 6

A t 9 AM the next day, the doctor finally came in. "Hello, Mr. Hall. I am Dr. Cole. I have a few questions to ask you. First of all, do you know where you are?" "West Valley psych unit." "Do you know what year it is?" "Huh?" "What year is it?" I told him the year. "What day of the week" "I don't know." "Okay, that is fine", "Okay, my last question is: Why are you here?" "I'm schizophrenic." "Why do you say that, and what does that mean to you?" "I don't know." Actually, I knew, or had a hunch at the time about what this was about, but had not quite gotten a handle on it.

"What is your drug use?" he asked. "None" I said. "I do not drink." "We are going to do some blood work on you now." And the doctor left the room. Soon a nurse appeared with some sort of needle. I was so terrified. "What are you doing?" I decided that it was time to just let them do what they wanted to do. I could escape later. I would be free again sometime in the future, but for now they had me trapped.

She inserted the needle and took blood. Then she inspected my arm and hand, which I had wrapped in towels. She threw the towels in the medical waste bin, disrespectfully. "You really did a number on yourself," she said. "It was an accident." "Sure," she said. "You cut almost all the way through your tendon. Why did you do that?" "The door was locked and I had to get inside."

After the nurse had finished putting the bandages in place, the doctor soon returned. "Stan, we have you here on psych hold for attempted suicide and psychotic symptoms. We are treating you with medicine to control the symptoms and also to prevent infection. We will be watching you closely. You are in a locked facility. You cannot leave during the 24-hour hold time - at least 24 hours. You also have to face the magistrate for the assault charges."

"My God," I thought, "It is all becoming clear. They want to destroy me, and it is all because of that fat jerk father of mine, Bill. He is the head of this thing. They are going to fry my brain with drugs so I will be pliable and easy to handle like a, like a sheep." I wondered if they really had a deeper agenda, which was not known to me at the time. One clue was that my entire arm, from the armpit to the hand, was wrapped in a big bandage so it couldn't move. They were going to do something like mummify me.

I played along. "Thank you, Doctor, for providing me with bandages and medicine. I'm sure those other symptoms, whatever you call them, are a misdiagnosis. I have a lot to do in my life and it will be great to get out of here." "Just a minute. I said a minimum of 24 hours, and then you have to face the magistrate," he said in a huff. "Okay, okay, whatever," was my reply. I was catching on. I was playing the game.

"Well it's time for the morning introduction for the new patients. It is time for you to leave your room," said Dr. Cole. He led me out to the main area where patients and staff were gathering.

A gray-haired nurse said, "This is the one and only welcome-to-the-facility talk that you will get. This is a locked unit and you cannot leave. Many of you are under court order to stay here and the rest of you are on some sort of legal restraint. Breakfast is served from 8 to 9 AM, lunch from 11:30 to 12:30, and dinner from 5:30 to 6:30. Snacks are also available. Are there any questions?"

"Where do we smoke?" said a 55-year-old, gray-haired, tattoo-covered biker type who was wearing a leather vest. "Outside on the patio only. And that is only from 7 AM until 8 PM." He screamed at her, "Fuck you and your rules." She got angry. "Scott. You do not want to be in restraints, do you?" "No ma'am," he replied meekly. He was faking submissiveness. It was a game. He was playing a game with her.

"Furthermore, I should mention, this is a men's facility. Spouses and family visits only between the hours of 10 and 11 AM. And 3-5 PM." "OH MY GOD!" I thought, "They are going to bring in a woman for me to have sex with! That's what they are up to. This is some sort of breeding pen." Things were clearing up slightly.

I knew that I needed more answers. But where could I find them? As the group broke up, I went up to the nurse and asked if I could have my book now. "Oh yeah, you were the patient that was reading Nietzsche," she said, and disappeared through a door. She reappeared with my book. I took it into my room. The book had a certain levity, a lightness to it. I almost floated while I carried it.

Nietzsche said it all. He was a genius among geniuses. "That which does not kill me makes me stronger." Oh, boy, I thought, was I getting stronger by the minute. Then he states: "I am an authority now, because no one really understands me. Long after I am dead will my words no longer be authoritative, they will just be seen simply as the truth." "That's me," I thought. "It is only people in the future who will know my thoughts to be the truth."

Then he explained how the world really works. "Walk on a worm, and he acknowledges that this is how things should be. In the words of a moralist, this is called 'humility.' But the role of the thinker today is to take shots at morality, just as an anarchist shoots at royalty." My whole body tingled reading his words. I really thought he saw through everything, right to the very core of reality. I decided at that moment that I was a thinker, a new philosopher, too.

Morals are created by religion to control people. All laws are created by rulers, in order to hold us down. What the rulers fear is that we will wake up one day and see that there is no need for God or religion, or even for them. That is why they invest so heavily in forcing religion on us: to keep us down. That is, those of us who would rule if the veneer of lies were removed.

The majority of the people want simply to be herd animals, and they believe in the illusion of religion to make them feel comfortable. The things they call "good" are the codes of conduct of herd animals or of slaves. Don't rock the boat. Get along. Be nice. But no leader has ever had to live by these rules.

As religion goes away, thoroughly and completely crushed by science, these rules will crumble, taking so-called civil society with it. Rulers will try increasingly harsher tactics to enforce the old order, the order that is lost when God is dead. He knew. Nietzsche knew all this. He was writing for me as my life is now, I thought. He was speaking to me.

I began to see the world as I thought it truly was. In the modern era, the rulers have put in even more controls on us to compensate for the end of religion. Most of it is the nonsense on television and on the radio, I thought. When TV and radio fail to control us they put us in psych units and tie us down and put us in restraints. That is what they were doing in this place. Then they would breed me like some sort of dog so that I would join the system and just be a normal slave or herd animal.

I will play along, I thought. I made up my mind to let them think that their lies made sense to me. I figured that they were probably watching me with cameras and speaking in secret code but I was still smarter than all of them.

They were serving lunch. I stopped reading and played along with them and pretended to follow the rules: to eat lunch like a hamster in a cage. At lunch, the tattoo-biker was making more of a fuss. He wanted to smoke during lunch. He had made some friends in the unit that were backing him up. They all wanted to smoke during lunch. I waited in great anticipation to see if these scum would cause a riot.

"No smoking inside!" yelled one of the staff. The biker had a fit. "Goddamn it!" He threw his lunch plate with all its food right through the window in the side of the dining room. Patients were screaming. One man started running away. All the staff ran in towards the biker and grabbed him, dragged him to the ground, and climbed on him to hold him down. The head nurse came out, the one with the gray hair. "Scott, you are not going to like this."

They led him off down one of the side corridors and through a set of double doors.

The nurse announced in a loud voice, "Okay everyone, just finish your lunch and we will clean up the mess when lunch is over." Everyone was so nice all of a sudden. We played nice. I was nice.

After lunch, the medical tray came out. "All right, everyone line up. It's med time." I wondered what was going on. "Stan Hall: Mellaril, Haldol, Ciprofloxacin." There were three little pills in a paper cup for me to swallow. The dispenser nurse said, "Swallow them now, in front of me." I played nice and pretended to swallow, then quickly walked to my room where I spat out all three pills. I was winning. They could not make me into a herd animal.

Back in my room, the book continued to reveal itself as incredible. I have never learned so much between the covers of a single book in such a short period of time, I thought. Nietzsche had also given me personal guidance for my life. He said, "The formula for happiness in life is to have a goal and a straight line to reach it. The goal is always derived from basic instinct, not from any virtue." I just need to understand my basic instincts, I thought, and find a goal based on that, and a plan to achieve it.

People outside were laughing at me. But I did not care anymore.

Tuesday, Day 7

O fficer Randles was there at the front entrance the next afternoon, to take me to jail and to court. My court appointment was at 3 PM and he was there at 1:30. All the release paperwork took about a half hour, giving us a full hour to make it to the courthouse.

The officer was driving, of course. I was caged into the back of the car by a metal screen, and there were no door handles on the insides of the rear doors. I asked him, "How do I get out if there is a fire in the car?" He replied, "You don't get out. You burn." Then he started that chuckle he had, the one I had heard before. I did not respond. Then there were several minutes of silence.

"Stan, I am sorry you lost your mother. Debbie told me about it. Your mom was a really fine human being." I just sat there and thought about how I am going to miss her. He started talking more about how he had actually known my mom for quite a while and had visited her at her house. He was telling a story about what her neighbors thought, having a cop car parked in her driveway, and he started laughing. I was not really listening and did not get the joke.

At the courthouse, no one was laughing. They were just scared. Just a minute, I thought. They were going to bring me a wife and make me breed, but that never happened. Maybe this would be it. Sitting there, I grew cold.

Officer Randles led me to the magistrate. My mother's lawyer was there, Mr. Schultz. I guessed he was my lawyer now.

The charges were read: "Breaking and entering, assault, wanted for questioning in unrelated homicide. Mr. Hall has completed his psych eval and 24-hour hold after a possible suicide attempt. Tox screening at West Valley shows positive for amphetamines." Then the judge said, "Do you understand these things?" I told them what the system wanted me to tell them: "Yes, I do."

"I have assigned you to spend the next month at the Oxford House. It is a halfway house that will require you to leave the unit every day and look for work. You must not drink or use drugs. There will be random drug tests and you must be inside the house between 8 PM and 6 AM. Do you understand this?" I almost laughed out loud. They wanted to put me in a cage. "Yes, I do."

I thought, "What was this shit about not drinking? I will not drink no matter what they do to me. Drinking is for slobs. Drinking is for scum like those winos in the jail. Who do they think they are talking to here?"

"One last thing" said the judge, "you are not allowed within 1000 yards of 605 Circle Drive, Apartment B, East Palo Alto, or 1126 Springer Road, Los Altos, or any other place where your father is. You are also not allowed within 1000 yards of 1187 Hamilton Avenue, Palo Alto, the residence of Karen South." That was ridiculous to me. "1126 Springer Road is my house," I thought. I was sure this was some sort of test to see if I would submit to the system and surrender what is rightfully mine in the name of subjugation. What I was thinking was "I will kill that SOB – that fat slob – Bill. That's my house."

What I said was, "Yes, your honor."

I turned around, and Mr. Schultz wanted to talk, "I'm so sorry about your mother's death," he said. I cut him off. "I didn't do it! I swear I did not do it!" "I'm not saying you did," said the lawyer. I tried to think of what the proper herd-animal code words were to answer him. "Thank you for your concern." Then I turned away. Officer Randles drove me to Oxford House. Along the way in the cop car, he said to be sure to follow all the instructions of the court, and everything would be fine. He was probably a part of the overall scheme to cage me. I wondered if anything he said was actually true: for instance, did he actually know my mother?

Having no transportation, I needed a set of wheels. My truck was impounded again, this time in Santa Clara. Since I still had money, I could afford to pay the cab fare. The impound site would be open for just about another hour. I stopped inside the Oxford House to look up the phone number for the impound site. I called the place using my cell phone, which I still had at the time.

After the impound site released my truck, I was out on the road again. They hadn't been able to break me or make me into their herd animal. They hadn't been able to make me drink. Son of a bitch, hell yes! It was off to the shop. It was just about closing time and Midge was there along with Bart and Curt, and also their father, George. It was unusual for George to be there.

I was all smiles and hellos. On the other hand, they did not seem to think it was a great idea to see me like this. It was rare for George to speak, but he said, "Stan, our attorney has advised us to not have contact with you for the time being until this case is completely over and done with. Bart has to go to court in another week. We would prefer that you would just stay away for at least that amount of time."

I was stunned and did not really know what to say. What were they talking about? Bart was innocent. The shooting was indoors, which was legal. I was just helping out. "What is going on?" I asked. George said, "Please just leave now, we cannot talk to you."

I turned around and walked over to my truck. As I got into the car, I glanced back over to them and none of them were even looking in my direction.

I could not think any good thoughts after departing. What had happened to my friends? Was George behind all this? Or Midge? She's the one who had all that religion in her. Still, it did not make sense.

Ross's house was next. He was happy that I was out of the psych unit and that he had gotten his motorcycle back. I asked him, "Ross, where did you get that book *Beyond Good and Evil*? It is incredible. It explains everything." He was puzzled. "Oh. I am just renting and the owner left some of his books here. There are a bunch more of those titles." I felt a shock like lightning. "MORE?" "Where??" He led me into a side room, which was like some sort of library. There were all sorts of books by all sorts of people. And about ten books by Nietzsche. There was one called *The Antichrist*. One called *Twilight of the Idols,* another called *Joyful Wisdom*. Then there was a curiously named one. It seemed to be his autobiography and was titled *Ecce Homo*. Since it was just about the thinnest book on the shelf, I thought I simply had to read it.

I turned around and Ross was in the other room with Jonathan, measuring out some large quantities of marijuana. He offered me a bong hit and I said no, it would just make me get sleepy again. "Jonathan," I asked, "Do you have any more buzzy stuff?" "Sure, how much do you want?" "How about another twenty pills for fifteen bucks?" Then I thought again. "How about 40 pills for 30 bucks?" He said, "I don't have that many. I have to get a resupply." "Okay, then 20 for 15." We completed the deal. I took five and started reading the book.

And what a book it was. This man had struggled and struggled with all sorts of illnesses and people who were out to get him and put him down. He said the role of religion is to simply keep the weak in their miserable state so they will be dependent and slaves. It is only by overcoming suffering that one can become strong. Right on. They are trying to make me suffer. I will stay strong. Nietzsche had simply awesome things to say about food and drink. He said to stay away from strong meats and from sausage. You will just end up like the German people, who are stupid and pathetic. And alcohol. Never drink alcohol. That is half the reason why the German people are lazy, degenerate and incompetent. The only things that make that country even function are the immigrants from Poland and France. He was telling it like it is. Alcohol completely finishes off a civilization after religion has done the initial damage with its "Christian morality" and other false belief systems.

His ideal man for the new era after the death of God is a hero: a superman who does not need false belief systems and lives a real life based on the real world as it is, not some made-up dogma. This new man, the superman, will rise above the herd to shape the future for a stronger, better world and leave the old false ideas of "God," "democracy," and "equality" behind.

A superman. Behold the superman. THAT IS IT. They knew that about me, and they were trying to stop me. That's what that psych unit was about, the phony arm bandage. I had discovered that they were trying to destroy me.

Karen could see I was a superman and picked me to make a child who would be a member of the new class of leaders that Nietzsche was talking about. She knew. She saw. I am superman. She is superman. And Sean will be a superman. It all became clear.

I don't think it took me more than three hours to finish the thing.

With this new understanding, I thought, I will never make such a stupid mistake as to listen to any so-called 'expert' again. What a fool I was to ever listen to anyone.

Wednesday, Day 8

Driving away from Ross's house at 3:30 AM it was perfectly clear that I was always meant to be a superman, and that everyone knew it too. They want to suppress me. They want to make me drink, and lower me down. Not drinking is the sign of a superman. Alcoholics Anonymous, which is full of people who do not drink, is a poisonous conspiracy to destroy potential supermen who are not drinking and fill their heads up with slave morality and bullshit Christian morality. Crap like "we are all equal before God." Karen has totally been taken out of the superman life by that slave society. She has sold out to the herd. It all started when they gave her those pills. Antipsychotic, they call them. That is what they tried to do to me. It's just the first step towards enslavement.

I did not need any of those pills, I thought. I just need the buzzy pills - Adderall. I was going to drive all night.

The first stop was the 7-11. Sunflower seeds were all that I would eat starting right then. And I would drink only pure water. I needed a hunting magazine to learn about the new guns they have out now. F-ing cops took my deer rifle after the ambush. What the hell was Rudy doing there anyway? That stupid asshole.

I headed north, towards the city. I went up Highway 101 towards the Golden Gate Bridge. It took a while to get across the city, even at 4 AM. A parking spot near the bridge will suffice. I was all by myself. It was wonderful! The bridge was open and I could walk across. I ran across. My body was just flying along as I ran. How far is it down to the water? About a mile, I guessed. I told myself, "Superman can fly, the one in the comic books. That kind of superman I have not yet become, but I will! Amazing freedom! Incredible to be out here!!"

Getting all the way across the bridge took almost no time. What is on this side? Okay, I was on my way back. Maybe I will just sleep in my truck, I thought.

A couple of hours went by and there was too much noise to continue sleeping. My mouth was seriously dry but there was plenty of fresh water in the cab to take care of that. There were some public restrooms available to take care of the call of nature. I was back on the road.

Oh God, life is so great. Thank you, God, for Nietzsche! "Ha, Ha," I laughed at my joke.

The most important thing to do is get a good supply of buzzy pills. I needed to talk to Jonathan about a good supply. But where was he? I called Ross on my cell phone but there was no answer. It was 11:00 in the morning on a weekday. Ross was teaching school. I thought that Jonathan was also a teacher, but at an elementary school. That's right. Berry School.

If you drive down Springer Road, in Los Altos, to Berry Street, then turn left; on the left is Berry School. There was plenty of parking in the lot. I wonder which classroom Jonathan is in? I'll just go to the front desk, I thought. "Where is Jonathan teaching? Which classroom?" The lady behind the counter said, "Do you mean Jonathan Bickford? He is in room 10, but class is going for another 15 minutes before lunch."

I waited outside the classroom for the next few minutes until the kids started pouring out. They were probably first graders. Then I walked in. "Jonathan!" I said. He had a look of horror on his face. I continue, "Hey, I want to talk to you about something." He was totally silent for a while; then he said "How about after school?" I let him know that I wanted to buy in large quantities, now, so if he could just tell me where his supplier was, I would go there and leave him alone. There were still a few kids in the classroom but they were not listening. He said, "His name is Clancy. He is at the corner of Pulgas and Weeks, East Palo Alto, every night around 6 PM – now get the hell out of here!" "Thanks!" I said, walking out. I did not know why he had to get so ticked off at me.

Next stop was the bank. Down Middlefield Avenue to Palo Alto, a few miles before Oregon Expressway, is the Wells Fargo Bank. The ATM would not give me enough money, so I walked into the bank and asked for a withdrawal. There seemed to be guards all over the place. The people are all staring at me. They are mumbling about how I have such lousy clothes on, that I do not know how to dress well, especially considering I have so much talent and have so much money. I told the cashier to give me a complete withdrawal of my account and showed her my ATM card. After a few minutes, she returned with a little over three thousand dollars in cash and counted it out in front of me. I said thank you and I was on my way.

Maybe those people were right, maybe I need new clothes, I thought. There is the Stanford Shopping Center just down the roadway, and I would not be going to East Palo Alto for at least four more hours. Just getting a few of the Adderall pills into me would make the whole thing fun.

Macy's has escalators. I had forgotten that – I had not been inside Macy's since I was just a kid. I felt like a kid again. I wanted to look at the toys. Little Tonka toys – Hilarious!

Now, how about a men's suit? I can just get one that is not tailored, standard sized slacks, XL pants and jacket, size 18 shirt, blue of course. It all seemed to fit pretty well considering that I am, well, a little overweight. I would need a good tie to go with all this. I did not spend more than two hours picking out all these new clothes, and I wore them out of the store. The total cost was only about $550. However, I did need new shoes to go with the outfit and that cost another $150, but that was no big deal.

I went back to the store and bought a cute little yellow truck for Sean. It was a Dodge like his Daddy's. When I had gotten back to my truck, I sat in my Dodge in the parking lot. The toy was so cute I just had to open the box and take it out. I laughed and laughed.

There were still about two hours until I had to be in East Palo Alto, and it was so wonderful to have the chance to see Sean again. A drive up Oregon Expressway to Middlefield, left to Hamilton Avenue, to that little white house three blocks down. Karen's car, a

Hyundai, was in the driveway. She never had any sense in cars. Anyway, this time she would be happy to see me.

She came to the door, and opened it to find me walking through, a big smile and Tonka toy in hand. "Hi Karen!" I was at the top of my game. "What the hell are you doing here?" "I have a toy for Sean found it at the Stanford mall." "Why the hell are you dressed in a fucking suit?" she asked. It was the perfect setup question. "I am dressed as the new me. Do you like it?" "You are just a fat slob in a suit now." "Karen, don't be mean. Let me see Sean." She halted and looked me in the eyes. I looked back at her and noticed she had not dyed her hair in a few days so the roots were sticking way out. "You are loaded!" she said with a scream. "What the hell are you on? Meth?? Crack??" Such a question was not worthy of being dignified with an answer.

"Don't you remember I have a restraining order on you? I order you out of here. Get the hell out!" She took a step towards me. The bitch. I would not yield my ground to this psycho bitch. "I am seeing Sean now." I yelled, "Sean! Its Daddy!!" He was only about six years old and he managed to come out of his room and look at me. "I have a present for you!" Karen was silent. "Here it is Sean, a Tonka toy." He loved the toy and said thank you thank you thank you, over and over. It made me so happy I could cry. "Daddy has to go now." I looked at Karen and she was ready to explode. She said to Sean, "Say goodbye to Daddy and go into your room." He did so and Karen grabbed me by the shoulder and took me out in front.

"You lousy, no good, slime ball! Look at what you are doing to Sean!!" She caught her breath.

"He barely sees you, and when he does you are loaded. Look at what you have done with yourself. Killing an innocent man at that stupid machine shop with your stupid buddies – and now you come by here loaded!" Then she continued, "And wearing a stupid suit – you never could do anything right! Just look at you!! You got a perfectly good degree from Berkeley and you cannot earn a decent living. You fucked up the only job you ever had by trying to be some sort of fucking hero. You have barely made any child-support payments. The whole goddamn world would be better off without you!"

She grabbed me by the shoulders and spun me around and pushed as hard as she could. Karen is a pretty big girl and she pushed hard and I damn near fell over. "Fucking kill yourself asshole! Kill yourself!" She yelled it over and over: "Kill yourself!" I remember my arms tingling and my chest having some pain. It was so sickening to listen to her. "Suicide!" "Kill yourself asshole." I ran down the driveway but that did not help because she ran after me yelling "kill yourself, kill yourself"

I opened the pickup truck door and got in and closed the door. She was still yelling, so I turned on the radio full volume while I drove away. The oldies channel was on, and the announcer said that next we are going to hear another Beatles classic, "Helter Skelter," followed by "I Get By with a Little Help From My Friends." What a relief, I thought, as I drove away. The

Beatles were there for me when no one else was. Then Helter Skelter came on and after the opening few words John Lennon was singing "Time to kill." "Time to Kill." "Time to Kill." He was in on it. Karen and John Lennon. No. That cannot be - John Lennon is dead. The radio station is in on it. They changed the words. They are commanding me.

I pulled over, and turned the radio off. The words to "Helter Skelter" were playing over and over. I get it: Karen is Sharon Tate. She wants revenge for what they did to her. I cannot quite decipher the message. What does this mean?

I was thirsty as hell so I drank a Diet Coke. There is no way I will ever drink alcohol again. Can you imagine what would happen if I did? The world would lose a superman. Everything I have ever stood for and fought for would be lost. Sean would never get the training he needs to be a ruler.

It was already past six o'clock, and I needed to drive across University Avenue to the other side of the freeway to some place called Pulgas Boulevard. I had a feeling it was going to be a long night. How many more of the brown pills do I have? I turned on the interior light and pulled them out. There were only five left. I put on my glasses and looked closely at them. There were little initials on them. They said HS098. Wonder what that is. I rinse them all down with Diet Coke.

Speeding away in my faithful Dodge truck, I was careful to stay inside the speed limit. It was not a good time to get a ticket, because Karen would use it against me. I needed some music and had better try another radio station. The Supremes are on a different channel. No more oldies. They are all in on it. News channel. The announcer says, "hundreds of civilian casualties in the war zone this afternoon." I could not stop laughing. University Avenue in East Palo Alto was what they called the "war zone" when I was in high school ten years ago. The radio continued " streets are empty and military patrols are out." I looked out the window and there were cop cars everywhere, and also many black women in metallic clothes and blonde hair. There were also a lot of black guys just walking the streets. What a place. The old me would have been so scared here. This was nothing to me now.

I came to the end of the road, a T-intersection. In the distance there was a four-story building that said "Facebook Research Center" on the front. What is that message? I burst out laughing. Cannot stop laughing.

I made a U-turn at the signal, went back down to Bay Road, made a left, then to Pulgas, then to the next corner. There was a little beer joint there called "Andy's." Why would I be afraid of going into a beer joint? What could possibly happen??

A young black girl of about – who knows – 17 walked over to me. "Y'all lookin' for somthin'?" I say calmly "Clancy." She started giggling. "Clancy – He's a friend of mine!" She puts her arm around mine and we go into Andy's. Fucking cigarette smoke. They want to poison me with booze and kill me with cigarette cancer. I will not be afraid. She sat me down next to Clancy. "Hey Buddy, what you want?" He looked at my suit. "Brand new suit, huh? What can I do for you?"

"I want Adderall and I have $2500 with me. Get me all you can." He looked at me calmly and said, "You a cop?" I got so angry. "What the fuck are you talking about? I hate cops." I caught my breath. "I am a superman." "Superman?" said Clancy. "Well how about that? Well, you need to know that you can get about 50 bags of 50 brown birds for that amount of cash. Show me your cash. I pulled out the money and show it to him. He said, "You're cool... Okay, well, I got to round the stuff up. Why don't you just spend about an hour with Stella here while I take care of my side of the deal." Stella. That must be her name.

Clancy put his arm around my shoulder and led me into the parking lot. I have a new friend. He's probably a superman too. Stella is a wild woman and I can stay a superman and still get something out of it.

"Why don't you drive Stella over to her place and we will see you back here at eight?" That sounded like a great deal. Stella got into my vehicle giggling and giggling. We went back up to Bay Road again, then turned left, then a few houses down we were at her place. I put the truck in park, got out, and noticed something crunching under my new shoes. It was still light outside so I looked down. I had just stepped on a syringe. "Stella is a carp," I thought to myself. "A bottom fish." This is what supermen do. We keep slaves. I said it, "She is my slave for the next hour." I started laughing so hard I could not stop. She said, "What's the madduh wid u?" I said "Nietzsche!" She said, "Dude, you crazy. Nee Chee, huh?" Who cared if she could pronounce the name - she was mine for an hour.

We walked in and there was some more crunching along the way. Dog shit smell in the front yard. Door unlocked so we just went in. Did not smell so bad inside. Only like mold or mildew or something. "You want to get high?" she said. Then she took it back, "You is already too high!" I did not quite know what she was talking about.

She led me into the other room where there was a bed. "What you want?" I said, "You know." She said, "I mean what you want first, a suck or what?" She took off her clothes and jumped on the bed. This, I thought, was the way it should be. I took off my new suit, including the tie and the new shoes, and got in bed with her. This was good and things were just right. She had needle marks on her arms and her blond wig fell off the side of her head. It was great to get into her. She said, "You are so good!" Then she started laughing.

After about a minute the door swung open so I flipped over and looked. It was Clancy and a few of his friends from the bar. I stood at the edge of the bed. "We have a message for you, superman." Then he hit me as hard as he possibly could right in my stomach. I would have screamed if I could, but he knocked the wind out of me. "How that feel, superman?" Stella was laughing hysterically, while Clancy came over to me and landed a few in my face. Then he started kicking me in the stomach. I was coughing and coughing and choking and could not get up. He put his shoe on my face. "You get your muthafuckin' ass outta here from now on."

I looked over to the other side of the room and Clancy's friends had my clothes and they were going through the pockets, taking everything and putting it into their pockets. Lying on the floor, I could not help but throw up. Clancy, Stella and all their friends departed quickly.

There were no sounds after that except distant sirens, car sounds and some distant music. By now it was very dark and I could not see too well. I found a light switch and turned it on, but no lights came on. I crawled around on the floor. They had taken all my clothes. My hand found my keys on the ground. No clothes. Nowhere. It seemed reasonable to sit and plan out a way to get out of there. I sat there for quite a while.

Thursday, Day 9

This is all part of the test. My face was a mess. I could not even see out of one eye. My right hand, where there had already been a huge injury before, was gushing blood. The bandage had been torn off and I could not find it. Indeed, a test. Karen, Bill and Jonathan had commanded Clancy to do this to me to try to derail me on the way to becoming a leader. This indeed was a "message for superman."

I wrapped the bed sheets around me, looking like an ancient Greek and walked out to the Dodge. Key in ignition. Lights on. Pause. Let me look in the mirror. I could barely see my face behind the blood. Enough of that self-pity shit, I thought – it is time to get going.

I make the Dodge do a U-turn on Bay. Then I drove out to University Avenue and made a left. The cops had blocked the road off. What is this? There was a long line of cars going up to a barricade in the road where the police were talking to people. "OH GOD! Sobriety checkpoint – this is hilarious," I thought. There were a few more cars in front of me before I had to talk to the cop. I had nothing to hide, I figured; I would just remain calm and let the officer know that I don't drink at all.

Finally, it was my turn. He asked, "Have you had any alcoholic beverages tonight?" I looked at him right in the eye. "No – I quit drinking a long time ago." For some reason he did a double take. "Sir, where are your clothes?" "I lost them." "What happened?" "Nothing."

"Please step out of your vehicle." I got out and wrapped the sheet around me. Standing with bare feet, I told him, "I'm going to a costume party." He then asked, "What day is today?" I said, "Halloween, of course," just trying to lighten things up. He was being far too serious about this thing. "Please stand over here." He radioed in something about a "whack job." I figured that meant he knew about Clancy and Stella and Jonathan and what they had done to me. A "whack job" must be police talk for the robbery. They had seen it before and they knew I needed some temporary protection. Certainly they believed in the old-fashioned moral arguments about not taking other people's property. That is what Clancy had done to me. Cops are basically just herd animals. They are like sheep, but they enforce the herd mentality on the other sheep. I figured that when they found out I was a leader, not a herd animal, they would just let me go.

Another officer arrived and said there were three warrants. "What is your name sir?" "Stanley Hall." "That matches the license plate for the owner of this vehicle. There are three outstanding warrants on you, Stan." Goddamn it, they have sold out. I decided to be brave. "Who put you up to this? Was it Karen or was it my Dad?" Right then, I unfortunately lost my cool after looking down at my thumb, which was gushing blood down the sheet I was wearing. "It was both of them. Confess! You are working for both of them!!"

I ran right at them, which was probably a miscalculation. One lesson I learned that night was that you should never, ever try to get a cop to confess in front of other cops. Instead, one of those black bastards in the blue suits pulled out a billy club and hit me right across the back. The handcuffs were on me again and they dragged me over to a cop car. My sheet was left lying on the ground. They were just trying to humiliate me. Taking my sheet away was a crime against me. I have rights. "Give me my sheet! My sheet!" I screamed – I was just trying to get them to be reasonable.

One of the cops did pick up the sheet and noticed all the blood on the front. He came over to the car and threw the sheet over me, saying, "We're getting EMTs." I leaned over to him and said, "It is fate that leaders always have to bleed." The asshole rolled his eyes up into his head. There were sirens and then the ambulance arrived and an EMT came over. The cops opened the rear door again and took me out. The guy looked at me and he just started laughing. The bastard was screeching while he looked at me. Then he said the strangest thing: "I am not trying to hurt you, so be still." What was he talking about?" I wondered. I let him look at my hand. Oh yeah. I told him, "My father was taking my house away from me. It was rightfully mine." He looked up and said, "Yes, I know." At last someone was straight with me. I let him fix the hand. It got a new bandage.

The cops discussed what they would do with me next. I was back in the car again and the windows were all rolled up so I couldn't hear. They were laughing. Laughing at me! I am the one who should be laughing at them. They started singing "Lucy in the Sky with Diamonds" and laughing. They huddled together while they planned what to do with me, giggling intensely.

After a few minutes of that, one of them stuck his head in the door and said, "You have to face charges downtown." That was code again. They were still laughing at me. I will have my own laugh. One of the cops, a black man, got into the driver's seat and starting talking on the radio. Shit, the cops were controlling the radio all along. That's how they communicated. It was tied into the oldies station and they had been watching my every move all along.

It was time for my laugh at their expense. "HELLO, COP!" He told me to sit still and be quiet. We were going to a "very nice place," he told me. I said, "You mean the KKK headquarters! I am the grand wizard of the KKK! HAR, HAR, HAR!" I was forcing the laugh to remind him of where he belonged. I started coughing. He just shook his head back and forth. He was probably trained to react that way.

He picked up the cop radio and started talking in code. "Wacko downtown," he said. That was not a very clever code. I said, "Put on the radio." He said nothing. Then I told him "I want to hear "All you Need is Love" by the Beatles. That was a trick I had learned by watching the movie "A Beautiful Mind." Don't let them know what you really want – tell them your second choice and pretend it is your first. John Nash was a superman. But the trick did not work. I asked the cop, "Didn't you see that movie?" He did not reply.

We went back to that place downtown. I was stuck again in the cage with 20 lowlifes. They were real stinkers this time. One guy was so drunk he just kept barfing and barfing in the toilet. I needed to pee. What the hell was I supposed to do? I would not be intimidated or bullied by the cops or the people they put in this cell. I just pulled it out of my pants and peed on the back of the guy's head. One of the other guys, another filthy drunk, came over and said, "What the hell you doin'?" I would have punched the guy but my right hand was mangled and in a bandage, and I needed my left hand to hold up the sheet. So I just peed on the floor. "You asshole!" the drunk shouted. This situation is so ridiculous, I thought to myself. The world is such a screwed-up place that a drunk, black-skinned loser would be judging me.

After about an hour they took me out of the cell and put me in a side room. They had some clothes for me to put on. The clock said 5:15. It was probably the morning. My hands were shaking for some reason and it kind of hurt my right hand. The clothes were too tight so I let them know. These fucking cops can't do anything right. The cop in the room said, "The clothes are just right. You are too fat." I put them on anyway but couldn't button the shirt all the way.

The cop put me back in the cage and said the judge would see me at 10 AM, so I can face the charges against me. It was some sort of play on words about my face being such a mess. He was just trying to shame me some more so I would become a herd animal. They would never break me.

The next thing they did was to let large spiders loose in the cell. They were black widows the size of baseballs. One of them was crawling over the puking drunk who was still at the toilet. He did not notice, so I refused to pay attention. Then several came at me at the same time. I shouted, "God is Dead!" at the top of my lungs and they ran. Those bugs are nothing but eight-legged sheep – looking for a shepherd.

My powers were growing during those four hours of waiting. With the power of my mind I was able to stop the guy from puking. Then I commanded him silently to stand up and look at me. He did. He stood there on the other side of the cell and looked right at me. He knew who I was. I was his master. He was my slave. I figured that this is how it would be from now on as I built up my flock of followers one at a time.

Damn if my stomach didn't hurt. I hoped that my new slave had not given me some sort of germ. God knows what they carry in them.

At about 10, the jail keeper came and got me. The overnight crowd had thinned out a bit by then. He took me through and we rode up the elevator to the second floor and stood in front of the courtroom doors as we waited our turn. Only about fifteen minutes passed before they led me into the courtroom.

The judge was named Patricia Maestes. "Your Honor," I spoke to her. She struck down the gavel and said, "Wait your turn. The charges against you from last night include drunk and disorderly conduct, assault of a police officer, public nuisance, malicious mischief. Do you understand these charges?" I said "Yes, but I do not drink." It was a chess game and I was winning right away. "Officers on the scene reported you as unable to walk a straight line." "It was a trick. They are trying to destroy me." She slammed down the gavel hard and said, "That amounts to a not guilty plea. Enter that into the record."

"Now we have the situation where you were ordered into a halfway house and the house said that you left the premises on the first day — that was four days ago — and you never returned. Judge Roberts has you on record as acknowledging that you would stay in the halfway house to avoid one year in the county jail. Do you understand these charges against you?" Oh no, she had pulled a move that I had not anticipated. They really were out to get me.

"I understand that I was supposed to stay there but I had to leave to conduct business." She replied, "You were unemployed and were to spend your daytime finding a job." I had never suspected that they would resort to manufacturing such blatant lies. She must be part of it all. Judge Maestes. She knows Karen, and my father, and probably Clancy too. I glanced around the courtroom, which was mostly empty. There were three cops there plus one lady clerk. My only hope was to run but there was no exit. I started laughing, remembering that had been the title of a book at Ross's house, right next to Nietzsche's *Ecce Homo*. It was a book called *No Exit*. This was hilarious. This was all a big chess game. Checkmate. I lose. "You win." I said.

She banged the gavel down. "This is not about winning and losing. This is about good and evil, and you are evil." I could not stop laughing at that. Good and Evil. How pathetic; she expects me to go back 200 years to when people believed in God and religion and good and evil. She hit the gavel down several more times. "There is no one here to post bond for you. You shall stay in the county jail until your hearing on the current charges. This is not scheduled for another two months."

"I want a lawyer. I have rights. You have violated my rights." The jailer came over and put me in handcuffs. "Quiet down," he said, "you are getting off easy." It was time to shut up. He was right. The jailer, whose name was Roy Goeller, led me out of the courtroom and into a police van waiting outside. Several other inmates were in the van with me. Roy closed the door and got in the driver's seat. I said, "Roy, I need my book." "What book?" he asked. I said that my book was in the cab of my truck. "It is called *Ecce Homo*." He said, "Well, it's in impound now. I'll see what I can do." He was such a nice guy. I cannot ever say enough about how important it is to have good friends.

Santa Clara County Jail is certainly not where I had expected to be after getting my masters degree in chemical engineering at Berkeley. But I was just one of those gifted kids who did not play the ordinary game that they expected of me.

Friday, Day 10

I began my first day by just watching TV. What they watch is so stupid. I could not even describe it to you. And the prison guards are even worse. They are probably drunk all the time when they are not here on shift. I guess one of them is OK. His name is Ben Norman. He has a little sense of humor, you know, about the blacks and Mexicans around the place. I want to tell you more about him later.

In county jail there are dorms that allow cross-mixing of prisoners among the general population. There is a day room for mingling, with chairs and tables. There is a large Plexiglas wall in the day room, which has some sort of wire mesh embedded in the plastic. On the other side are a couple of guards, who spend most of their time watching TV. Watching TV is what most people do when locked up in there.

My cellmate was this guy Leroy Gibson, who said he used to live on Bay Road in East Palo Alto. He is one of them. You know, like Clancy and Stella – a black. I didn't hate him because he was black. I never hated Leroy at all, even though, as you will see, we did not quite get along too well.

"What you in for?" I asked as we sat there in the common area. "My old lady put me here. She was banging some Mexican and I caught her so she called the cops." "What? You didn't do anything?" "Nothing." "Shit." "She told them about the stash of dope I had in the closet and they busted me for it." Kind of felt sorry for the guy but then again, he probably deserved it.

He had lived in East Palo Alto for about a decade and had spent a lot of time in the local lockup. The best job he had, when not in lockup, was as a parts puller in one of the local junkyards. He was there for a couple of months before they fired him for no reason at all. He laughed when he talked about his last day on the job when he went around breaking the windows on every car in the place.

I started to tell him about how I had a chemical engineering degree and he did not seem too interested. Within about ten seconds he began looking off to the other side of the room and became totally distracted. I stopped talking.

After a few minutes of just sitting there, I was restless too, and moved across the room to what appeared to be a bookshelf. There were a couple of issues of National Geographic magazine, a Bible, a few John Grisham novels, some James Patterson... There were some coloring books too. Wondered what they were doing there. Ross had really liked books. I wanted to talk to him.

Behind the Plexiglas wall there was the security guard, Ben Norman, in uniform. Billy club or nightstick at his side, he looked a little bored as he stared in at us twenty or so inmates in prison garb. His uniform was gray, and he had some sort of decoration on his chest. It looked like he was wearing combat boots or something, and that he spent at least seven hours a day lifting weights and working out. He had a big fishhook tattoo on his arm, and he said his nickname was Popeye when I talked to him through the little six-inch portal. I laughed, but he didn't act like it was funny.

He said he was a star college football player and was drafted into the pros, but did not quite make the team. The Baltimore Ravens had cut him in training and no other team picked him up. He had a degree in physical education from San Jose State College, and said it was pretty tough, having to learn all that chemistry and physiology. He was astounded when I told him I had a chemical engineering degree. "What the hell?" he said. "What are you doing here??"

I told him the whole story of how I had been employed at Fairfield and lost my job, was working in a machine shop for the younger brother of the guy who got me fired, and about the accidental shooting and the scuffle with my dad and with the cop. "You got screwed, Buddy," was all that he said.

Popeye said the most important rule was to never get caught smoking, or they would put you in solitary. Okay, I figured, I don't smoke anyway. "No fighting. No drugs, no alcohol." When he said the word drugs I thought about those little brown Adderall pills. Damn, one of those would do me some good right now. "Popeye, my name is Stan, glad to meet you" I said and walked away. He yelled at me through the portal, "Come back here!"

He said, "There is something else you need to know. Stay the hell away from a guy named Thomas. You will see he hangs around with another guy named Oscar, a huge black guy. Never do anything to upset either of those guys. And do not bother ever talking to any of the Mexicans. They are all in gangs and they want to kill you." My jaw must have dropped. "Did you hear me?" he said. "I heard you, thanks."

I went back to the cell and just sat there. Leroy was staring at the ceiling. I saw he was kind of reading a golf magazine. "Golf?" I thought to myself. "Hey Leroy, you play golf?" I asked. "Kind of, I used to play when I was a kid . . . not anymore though." Oh, I thought, he is just as bored as me. There is nothing else to do.

Leroy started complaining about his last cellmate. "This guy, named Jeffrey, was always talking down to me, you know, always putting me down. He was such an asshole - a real asshole. I am so glad he is gone." That reminded me of Bruce. Leroy and I had something in common.

He sat up in bed. "I have got to go now. I work in the cafeteria." I said goodbye and wondered how the hell Jeffrey had ever gotten out of this place. Leroy was out the cell door and I asked him, "How long until you get out?" He shouted over his shoulder "I don't know. There is a guy here named Dan who is helping me. White guy, brown hair, wears glasses."

I stayed in the cell for a while, thinking about what to do to get the hell out of this place. There were four tiny walls, two bunks, a toilet, and one drawer for all my belongings, which amounted to a toothbrush and a comb. Thank God the cell door was open during day hours. Speaking of God, where the hell is he now and why did I ever believe in any of that shit?

Outside the cell door it is about 50 yards down to the common area, where I had been talking to the guard. This time I went to see Dan. There he was, reading a book by himself. "Are you Dan?" "Yes, you must be Leroy's new cellmate." This guy was pretty sharp. "Yes, he told me about you. You are helping him get out."

Dan had a big smile. "My name is Dan Nelson." He leaned back and said, "Take a seat and tell me your story." Dan was an older guy, about 35 probably, with thin hair and a friendly way about him. He kept himself kind of neat, so to say, considering he was in a prison outfit. In other words, he didn't stink like Leroy.

I had already told the prison guard my story just a few hours before, so it was fresh in my mind. Dan got the brief version. He laughed when I told him about the fight with the black cop in East Palo Alto. "You are kidding?" I said no. Then for some reason I started telling him about Bruce, who had cheated me out of my job at Fairfield and who is now the associate director of the laboratory.

"Wait, wait, wait, stop right there." He said. "First of all, forget about Bruce and Fairfield and all that. You are in jail now. None of that matters." He was right. "The next thing you need to know is to never accept any plea bargain that they offer you. Always, and I mean always, demand a trial. No matter how good the deal seems." "What do you mean?" I asked. "The main problem that they face is the backlog of cases awaiting trial. They will do anything to avoid a trial, but you have a right to a trial. Insist – I mean insist – that you get a trial, no matter what. After they come back to you no less than three times, tell them that you may consider what they are offering, but insist that you are not guilty."

"I am not guilty?" I said. He said, "You are never guilty. Never. Always say that it was a mistake or that you were framed. Got it?" "Okay, thanks. I'll have to think about that," I said. It was just about time for the 5 PM dinner call. Inmates with last names with the letters H through N were to get in line first today. That meant both of us.

"We are lucky today, being first in line," he said. "Towards the end of dinner, the food kind of, you know, starts to smell bad." Tonight the food was stew.

We sat down in the eatery near the serving window. "OK, look at that guy, that is Oscar and the guy with him is Thomas. They are brothers even though they really don't look like it." I had noticed Oscar right away: a light- skinned black man who must have been six foot seven and three hundred pounds. I don't even know how they found a prison suit for him. Maybe they made it special. Thomas was about a foot shorter, darker skinned, shaved head. He was the one the guard had said to look out for.

Dan continued, "Oscar can get you anything you want here. You are his friend as of right now." "What do you mean?" I asked. "Anything," said Dan. "I want a woman." Dan laughed, "anything except for that. Oscar can arrange for any drug or substance you need, he can arrange things to work out your way or not your way, he can get you booze sometimes." There was a pause. "He can probably get you a guy if you want." I felt my throat tighten. "I hear you." Then he said, "The only thing you got to make sure of is that you don't cross up with Thomas. Now Thomas is another kind of fellow. He is no ordinary criminal.

"Thomas is in here for killing a man with a pipe wrench," said Dan with a pause. "He caved the guy's head in on the first blow and then just kept pounding until there was nothing left of the guy at all. When the cops arrived there was a pile of hamburger and Thomas just standing there with this pipe wrench. So they arrested him."

Something didn't make sense to me. "Just a minute, Dan, why is he in here? Shouldn't he be doing hard time somewhere, somewhere like Folsom or Chino?"

"He claimed it was self-defense." It was inside his garage and he claimed that this stranger had just walked into the shop in the middle of the afternoon and threatened to kill him. You see, it was a Sunday and there was no one else around, so there were no witnesses. He was just about to face a trial on murder charges, even though there was not a great case against him in terms of motive. At the last minute his lawyer talked him into accepting a plea deal for manslaughter charge. That's third-degree manslaughter, has only a 1-year sentence in county jail. So here he is." My throat tightened again. "If he had not listened to his stupid attorney he would have probably gotten off scot-free," said Dan emphatically. "That is what I am trying to say. Never, I mean never accept the deal and never admit guilt, no matter what." "But he killed a guy," I said. "That is not the point. He never should have admitted to anything." I was stupefied. I slurped my stew and rinsed it down with a glass of water.

"What about Oscar?" I asked. "Oscar was just a dope dealer who got in a jam," Dan went on. "He got ratted out by his girlfriend and the cops surrounded the house while he had a kilo of meth he was cutting up." "He was caught red-handed," I cried. "He tried to say that he did not know anything about the crystal, and that someone had just left it there. It was a good try but they had him pretty bad. Again, he accepted a plea deal because of the stupid lawyer he was assigned. He should have held out and demanded a trial." "Why?" I asked. "Well you see, when you go to the trial you can select jurors who will be sympathetic. He could have claimed the cops and his lousy girlfriend framed him. They might have let him off. You remember OJ, don't you?"

I said that OJ had the dream team of lawyers, for God's sake. "You don't get it, Stan – it was not the dream team that won the case. It was the incompetent prosecution that lost the case. Incompetence is an absolute guarantee on the other side." Wow, I thought, this guy knows his stuff.

"Just a minute," I said to him. I got up and walked over to Oscar's table and said hello to him. "Who are you?" said Oscar. "My name is Stan Hall. I am Leroy's new cellmate." By this time I had figured out that Oscar probably did not care that I had a chemical engineering degree from Berkeley. "You want something?" he said. I said, "Yes as a matter of fact I do, I want some Adderall. I heard you could get me some." "Get the hell outta here you little shithead. You got nothing that I want." Oscar was mean. I had thought he was the nicer of the two. "Okay, sorry." I walked away.

Dan had already left the cafeteria by this time, so I just kept walking past the table where we had been sitting, and out the door, down to the common room. All of this new information was getting me kind of tired out or something. I just wanted to sit down somewhere quietly. "Oscar thinks that I have nothing he wants" kept running through my mind.

Two men, one Hispanic-looking and the other white, were talking to a white guy about the Bible. "The message is clear," the Hispanic guy said, "salvation only comes through accepting Jesus as your savior."

"Okay, I understand," I said to myself while I listened in. "These guys are really sorry for what they have done and they need forgiveness. Of course, I can join in on this, and somehow make money to buy drugs." I decided to listen further, so I got up and sat next to them. "I am interested in what you are saying. My name is Stan Hall and I am new here." One of the white guys said, "My name is Robert and this is my brother Julio, and we are witnessing to our brother here... what was your name again?" "Pete," chimed in the other white guy. I get it. We are all brothers. "Pete, I am Stan, isn't this message great?"

"God is great," said Pete, "God is great. My dad was a minister and I just love this stuff." "He was?" said Julio. "My whole family went to church together every Sunday to Saint Mary's Church." Pete got a little hotheaded. "Saint Mary's? You are Catholic? Are you some kind of Pope lover?" That was my opening. "Pete, chill out. We are all one in Jesus, we just have some small disagreements." Julio added, "Yeah, I go to a Protestant church now, I mean I used to before I got in here." Silence. Then I spoke: "Everyone cool now?" Everyone nodded. "Let's move on. Where were you guys? Are we reading the book of Matthew?"

We continued on this old book for another hour, and everyone decided we'd had enough. There was a set of handshakes and then we said the Lord's Prayer. It was time to go back to the cell. On the way I passed the bookshelf and took the Bible with me. It was a large-print version with a thick, hardcover binding. Others would be impressed.

In the cell there was Leroy, staring at the ceiling again. Time to try it out. "Leroy," I said, "Listen to me." He turned sideways a little. "Leroy, you need to get God into your life." He screamed, "You been talking to Robert and Julio! Get the fuck out of here!" I could smell alcohol on his breath. Leroy was drunk!

How the hell did this happen? Where does he get the stuff, I wondered. Now I was really on to something. If I could get some booze I could trade it for the drugs that I need. "Sorry Leroy, I won't do that anymore." "Yeah," he said and went back to staring at the ceiling.

Now I began to plan. With this Bible, I can go cell to cell acting like I am converting the inmates. I can scope out each cell for where I can get some booze or pills. Damn, if I find pills, I can just slip them in the Bible. The booze will be a little harder.

It was dark and the cell door was closed. I lay there with my eyes wide open. There was no hope of sleep. In the quiet I could hear some of the other prisoners chattering, but that eventually faded away until there was the faint sound of crickets, making cricket sounds, "crick-crick-crick." Then silence. Leroy snoring. Silence. Crickets. Above me there was the sound of rats or something. They were chewing. "Crunch-crunch-crunch." Silence.

Saturday, Day 11

In the middle of the night, I got up and walked over to the front of the cell. There was some trash-talking going on outside. "You aint no nothing sonofabitch," and then "fag." Then "you are a freak-freak-freak-fag."

"Leroy, what are they saying?" I asked. "They are telling you to go to bed and shut up shithead."

In my bed again, I started thinking about my son Sean. "Where is he? Karen has kidnapped my son." Kidnapping is a crime. She is a criminal.

My mom, she loved Sean so much. I started to sob at the thought. "Mom I am so sorry you cannot see Sean ever again." "Shut up" shouted Leroy. "Fuck you, n..." – the n-word came out too quickly for me to catch it in time.

He flew out of his bed and came right at me. "Call me that and I will kill you. Kill you!" He grabbed me by the throat. All the prisoners in the cellblock were yelling, "Kill him! Kill him! Kill him!" They were all laughing and laughing. "Fight, fight, fight!" The lights came on. Leroy let go of my throat.

All the inmates were still yelling, shouting, and laughing. Both Leroy and I jumped into our beds and pulled the covers over our heads. I looked out with one eye and there was a guard at the set of bars looking into our cell. We were both perfectly still. After a few minutes the guard turned and walked away and the lights went out. The other prisoners slowly quieted down. Leroy was giggling. "I am going to kill your white ass tomorrow," he said. We both started laughing "he-he-he-he." The crickets were joining us "he-he-he." The rats also joined in "chit-chit-chit." Grinding their teeth together.

Where was my mom? She had died. It was my fault. I upset her so much by being put in jail and making her bail me out. "My God, what have I done, I killed my mom." I could hear her voice. "Lil scat," she used to tell me in Danish. It meant "little one." I cried and cried, silently, to myself only. Everyone is dead except my dad. "That bastard framed me. He broke the glass window in the back of MY house while he was occupying it. Then he hit himself in the head with the brick to fake the injuries. Then he called the cops. Hate him. Hate. Hate."

I must have slept for an hour or two because the whole place suddenly was very quiet. The only sound was from crickets. No rats. I could not get back to sleep. I have got to get some more Adderall, somehow, I thought.

There was a scheduled lawyer visit at 9 AM. He sat on one side of the Plexiglas window and I was on the other. He picked up the phone first and said, "Looks like you might be here for a while; no one is looking too kindly on you right now." I cut him off. "I did not do it! I was framed by that asshole!!" The lawyer, Mr. Schultz again, was a little startled. "The cop you attacked?" Oh no, I had forgotten about that cop. "His name is Chuck Branch, and he wants you to stay here," said Mr. Schultz. He talked about a hearing that had not been set yet, and a plea deal (that I was sure that I did not want). "I demand a trial," I told him and he started laughing. Why the hell was he laughing at me? This is serious stuff. "Who have you been talking to?" Silence. Then he continued, "Okay, okay, we may not accept their first offer. We do not know what will happen but Officer Branch is not too happy with you right now." I politely thanked him for his time. I never asked who was paying his fees.

The room for breakfast was again the same cafeteria from the night before, and I sought out Oscar and Thomas. "What youse want?" said Oscar with a sneer. I told myself "Oscar is your friend." Then I said, "Oscar, I want to be your friend." He said, "Yes I heard about that yesterday." I said, "What I offer you is salvation." You should have seen the look on his face. He was cross-eyed and his jaw dropped down on his chest. Oscar was so fat that he had a triple chin, not a double chin, when he looked at me. Then he started laughing hysterically. "You what? Ha-Ha-ha-ha-ha." Then Thomas started laughing too. I had not thought he even knew how to laugh. "Har-har-har," huge belly laughs. The laughter was so loud that everyone in the cafeteria wanted to know what was going on.

"I see you have been talking to Julio and Robert," said Oscar. I was caught. "OK. I want those pills. They are brown capsules. They are what I want." Then Oscar said, "There is something you can do for me. I want to know how Leroy gets his booze. You see, Leroy has been drunk for some time now and no one has quite figured out how he does it. I wouldn't mind sippin' a little hooch myself." I just said, "OK." He said, "You gonna do it?" I said, "Yeah, I will do it but you have got to give me a little sample first." He said, "No samples." Thomas chimed in, "No samples, no way. Get the info first."

Dan was across the cafeteria, and it was time for another visit. "Hey there new guy," he said, probably not remembering my name. "Stan Hall," I said, refreshing his memory. I said it so loudly that it seemed to echo off the walls. "Dan, you are friends with Leroy?" He said, "Well, as much as anyone can be friends in this joint." "Where does Leroy get his booze?" To that, Dan replied, "You'll have to ask him yourself – why would I tell you?"

"Dan, I can help you. I can save your eternal soul." His eyes almost popped out of their sockets. "Ha-ha-ha," he started laughing and he could not stop. "Oh, my God, this is too early in the morning," then he started slapping his knee. "Fucking nuts, you are totally nuts." I assumed that everyone was watching. "You get that from Julio and Robert?" Dan was red in the face from laughter; I think I was starting to cry. "There, there, little one," he said, "don't cry." That is what my mother used to call me, "little one."

We sat there silently for a few minutes. Then out of desperation I said "Dan, tell me your story." He immediately said, "I am an innocent man who was framed," and he hit his fist down on his knee. So I asked him, "Were you a lawyer?" He said, "No, I was a pharmacist. I went to pharmacy school, did all the right stuff, lived a normal life, had a happy home and then some DEA agents came into my place of business and arrested me." Then he continued. "They planted some evidence that I had been selling some illegal substances on the side." "Why did they do that?" I asked. He answered, "They were desperate to build up their careers and they wanted to catch a white-collar criminal and all the rest. They could not climb the ladder by just busting regular dope dealers, so they had to go higher up the food chain. They faked the whole thing." He rested with a grim smile on his face.

"Just a minute," I said, "you said DEA, that is federal. Why are you here?"

"Oh, yeah, I accepted a plea deal that my lawyer said that I had to take. It was for possession of a street drug – meth. The feds turned the case over to the State of California and I was sentenced under the state system. I should never – I repeat, never – have accepted the plea deal."

"So because of having a bad lawyer – who was as dumb as dirt – I am here and I lost everything: wife, house, car, business, freedom. That is why I am my own lawyer now."

"The state put me in Folsom Prison for a seven-year sentence, but the place was so overcrowded that after a year they moved me here to this county jail. They will probably send me back to Folsom at the end of the year to finish my sentence. Or they may move me to another county jail. I hope they do, in fact. Folsom sucks. It's really bad."

"You lost everything?" I said. I really felt sorry for the guy. "Yes, pretty much everything."

"Now let me tell you more about that bible stuff. Julio and Robert were two followers of a guy who used to be here named Manuel Javier Ruiz. He was the world's greatest Bible thumper, and could convert anyone. I mean anyone. He was great. Let me tell you this: guess what he called himself? He called himself Jesus. Jesus! And it worked. He would say it like the Cubans say it 'Hey-suesse' and he was converting everyone. He was a buddy of mine and I helped him with his legal problems. He stuck to his story that he was the anointed one – he did not believe a word of it – and they – in effect – let him go! The court ruled that he was a complete whack job, probably a psychotic, and he didn't even belong in jail. So they transferred him to a state mental hospital where he rapidly became completely normal. The hospital let him go in three months!"

"Dan, I need something." He was still telling the story. "Christianity can sure work some miracles sometimes. That was a miracle... Okay, what is it you need?"

"I need some Adderall. That's the stuff you were talking about. The DEA planted it on you to put you away. Can you get me some?"

"Oscar is your guy."

"Oscar will not give me any unless I tell him where Leroy is getting his booze," I said.

"I suppose I could tell you, but what do I get in return?"

"I could get you a job in a machine shop when you get out."

"Sorry, but as I told you, I am not seeing the outside for another five years at least, so no deal."

It was all so depressing as I got up and walked away.

Going down the hallway to my cell I ran into Julio and Robert. "Hey brothers!" I said, "Keep spreading the word!" Robert then said, "Stan, have you saved anyone yet?" To that I answered, "No, but I am trying!"

Back in the cell, I simply walked right up to Leroy and said, "Where do you get the booze?" To that he replied, "Shut up."

"I smell it on you."

"Why do you wanna know?"

I had to think of something. "Because I want some."

There was nothing but silence, and he turned away.

I sat there. What do I do? My mind is just screaming, going wild with sheer anxiety. I went back to the bookshelf. *A Purposeful Life* by Rick Warren. Christian stuff. Golf Digest, must have been returned there by Leroy. Another book was *Animal Farm* by George Orwell. Okay, I shall give that a try. Mr. Pig talking to Mr. Dog? Huh? What the hell is this?

There was a TV in the common room and the guard controlled the station. Oprah Winfrey was interviewing her special guest, Rahm Emanuel. I turned to the guy sitting to the right of me and said, "Who cares about Chicago, this is San Jose. Chicago is a million miles away."

"Rahm is a world-class phony, servant to the ruling class," was his reply. There was silence for a while. Oprah asked Rahm how his children were doing. It was so boring that I just had to turn to my neighbor again. "What are you talking about?"

"Rahm Emanuel is part of a set of puppets put forward by the ruling class of Chicago to try to keep the working class at peace. The workers of Chicago do not buy into what he is doing and will take action soon."

"What kind of action?"

"We, the working-class people who have fought the rich imperialist white man's battles in Iraq and Afghanistan to preserve capitalism, are trained in battle techniques sufficient to overthrow the bankers, the landlords, the billionaires, and all those who work for them. We have a large and quite sufficient arsenal that has been smuggled back from the war zones. The bourgeoisie do not know this. When the people speak through the barrels of their guns, the ruling class is going to be surprised."

"You are going to kill the rich people?"

"You had better believe it."

"You are going to kill Oprah?"

"We shall see about that. Some media celebrities have to be kept alive and re-educated for our purposes. Others, such as your hero Rahm, will be dealt with ruthlessly."

"What crime will he be tried for?"

"Who said there even was such a thing as crime? The very thought of a 'crime' is a construction of capitalism to keep the means of production in the hands of a few and away from the people. I say the only crime is capitalism itself."

"Killing people is wrong. You advocate killing people and taking their property! What are you, an animal?"

"No, my name is Geraldo."

I was a little lost for words, thinking maybe I had been rude to not formally introduce myself to Geraldo before talking to him.

"I am Stan Hall. I am in for assault. What are you here for?"

"They put me here to silence me."

It occurred to me that I had been warned not to speak to any Latino, because they basically wanted to kill me. I did not know he was one of them – a Latino - until he told me his name. Now Geraldo was indeed interested in killing other people. He just wanted to talk to me, not kill me, however.

"Geraldo, did you serve in Iraq?"

"No. And I am no servant."

"That was an interesting use of words, Geraldo. Have you heard of the book *Beyond Good and Evil*?"

"Nietzsche has been useful to us. You have been reading him, I see."

"You know him?"

"He is very dead. I used to teach philosophy at San Jose State. I was tenured faculty in Philosophy and Latino Studies. One of the classes I taught was post-modernist thought, and we started with him in the first week."

"Just a minute. You said he was dead?"

"Good God, man, he's been dead a hundred years! He's been dead almost as long as God has been dead," he said with a chuckle.

I told him passionately, "Nietzsche said it all. There was nothing left to say. There are those of us who are meant to be rulers and the rest are meant to be slaves."

"Which one am I?" said Geraldo, bursting out laughing. He laughed so hard he was slapping his knee, and drool was coming out of the corner of his mouth. Then he started coughing, and continued to cough for at least a minute.

"The ruling class has made me smoke too many cigarettes," he said with a grin, followed by another chuckle.

"OK, Stan, we now believe that Nietzsche got some things right. For instance, a few will always rule the many. That cannot be avoided, despite all you hear about 'democracy' and all that nonsense. But what we have now under capitalism is that one percent of the people have all the wealth. The other 99 percent have nothing and are locked up in jail."

I wondered if he realized what he had just said. But at least I understood what he was trying to say.

"Marx is the one you should be reading. It is as simple as this: we outnumber them. All we need is guns and the willpower. Then we do away with all of their racist, capitalist, Earth-endangering lies. The rest of this stuff, like the so-called great thinkers, are just distractions – distractions away from our class struggle – a struggle for justice and peace."

It seemed he thought that the world would be very peaceful after one percent of the population had been cut into pieces. "What are you saying, Geraldo?"

"I am saying that there will be peace only after justice. Justice is overthrow of the ruling class, followed by merciless punishment. The people will rule through elected panels, chosen for diversity in ethnic and cultural background, gender identity and race. Education will be the leading priority throughout the land. The people will live in peace in a completely Earth-friendly, sustainable economic system. Capitalism and greed will be no more."

"Are you going to put Bill Gates to death?" I asked.

"Oh my, oh my, you just don't get it," said Geraldo. Then there was silence again. He stared at the floor, and I waited.

After a while he spoke again. "It was such a waste of time being a college professor. The students were so clueless. The rest of the faculty – they - they - were such assholes. The pay was lousy. I had to live in a one-bedroom apartment because I could not even afford to buy a house. They made me pay for all my own expenses, like pencils and paper, because of the budget cuts."

Then, of all things, he started crying. It was embarrassing. I looked around the room and the Oprah show was having a commercial break for Carnival Cruises. A couple of guys were playing quarters in the other corner. The guard behind the Plexiglas was half asleep.

I went up to the guard and said through the little opening, "Do you have a Kleenex or something?" The guard reached into a box and pulled out a tissue and put it through the hole to me. I carried it over to Geraldo. He thanked me and continued to cry.

"Stan, do you know why I am in here?"

"No."

"I could not make ends meet on the shit pay they were giving me. This is Silicon Valley, for God's sake, and I make less than what a janitor makes at one of those places like Intel. I met a guy in a bar in Sunnyvale who told me he could sell me a half a kilo of cocaine at half the going rate. I could turn it around in a few weeks, selling to my students. So I cashed out my 403B retirement plan at the school and bought the half-kilo. On the way home from the deal the police pulled me over. The whole thing was a sting. They gave me two years in state prison for possession with the intent to distribute. They are just holding me here until they can free up some space at Chino."

It was getting more towards dinnertime, so I broke it off with Geraldo and said we would talk more, later on. I got in line a few people back from Thomas. "Hey Thomas," I said, "I hear the stuff you have is no good." He ignored me. I walked up ahead to his place in line. "I know where Leroy gets his booze." "What'd ya say?" "Booze, Leroy's booze." Oscar was right behind me. Right as I got to the front of the line and got my food, I walked away.

I sat down next to Dan. "I told Oscar and Thomas that I know where the booze is." Dan immediately said, "If you lied to them you are dead meat." To that I said, "Of course I lied. Now tell me where Leroy gets his stuff." "NO," was all he said.

"You have got to help me."

"Stan, you are in trouble now. You are going to have to give Leroy a hand job or something. He probably would like it. I don't know what else to tell you." Dan got up and walked away without finishing his food.

I sat there and Thomas walked up to my table and put his hand down. He said, "This is home-made Adderall." Then he walked away and where his hand was there was a little crystal roughly the shape of a cube, dark brown in color. I shoved it in my mouth and swallowed.

Walking back to my cell I heard Thomas' foot steps behind me. I turned around and he was not there. I went into the cell and the stuff was starting to kick in. I lay in my bunk and the jail cell was a fascinating place all of a sudden. There was still really nothing to do so I picked up the bible and started reading. Might as well start with Genesis. "This is a hell of a good book," I thought. "Wow. Every sentence is better than the last one." I was reading all about Noah landing the arc and the water receding so everyone was on dry land again. Noah is planting grapes and making wine and – wow – having a party!

The cell door closed. Thank you God that I am safe. The crickets were really loud and there was no way that I was going to sleep.

The rats, too, were clenching their teeth together, "cheech-cheech-grt-grt" and the crickets were saying "Leroy, Leroy, Leroy."

"Leroy," I said in a loud voice. "Whaddya want?" he said back. "I want some booze." "Asshole, shut the fuck up."

"Leroy, I am going to have the Mexicans kill you unless you give me some."

"Who may that be? Julio, I suppose?" says he.

"No, Pablo will kill you."

"He wants some?"

"Yeah, Pablo wants some but he doesn't know how to ask. He just knows how to kill."

Leroy handed me a little sandwich baggie that had some liquid in it. It had kind of a rotten smell but it definitely contained alcohol. I took the hooch and slid it into my little drawer. "I'll tell Pablo not to kill you." Then there was just quiet.

The crickets were chirping, "Kill him, kill him, kill him." The rats were grinding their teeth together, "You deserve this. You deserve this. You deserve this." It was amazing how much those rats understood.

"There is no Pablo," said Leroy. "You lousy sonofabitch. You got my hooch, you think you can get it for nothing?" He got up again, came up close to my face and said, "Blow me." The smell was awful. "Blow me, motherfucker."

I had no choice but to take the bible and smash it into his face. I screamed at the top of my lungs, "HELL NO!" Leroy's blood was all over the place, covering both my Bible and me. He yelled out at the top of his lungs and the fight was on.

He pushed me against the bunk bed and I hit my left arm hard against the little dresser. My right fist went into his nose where all the blood was coming out. God, did that hurt. My right hand was still all messed up from the fighting before. He tried a sucker punch, but I was too fast and blocked it, returning a sucker punch to his solar plexus, hitting full force. He picked up the dresser and threw it at me, missing.

The cellblock was in mayhem. All the prisoners were yelling again, this time with most of them cheering for Leroy. "GO, GO, GO, Leroy!" and "KILL, KILL, KILL!" The lights came on and the guards were inside in a flash. They had the cell door open in a minute and were all over the both of us.

I tried to stand up but the nightsticks were pounding on my back. "Stay down!" shouted one of the guards. Leroy was getting pounded too. The rats were screaming "Killem, killem, killem." After a few moments, they took me away down the corridor past some of the other cells. One guy yelled out "Did he fuck you, Whitey? Did he fuck you?"

We were pulled into the cafeteria, which of course was closed down, and entered a door inside and to the left that was usually locked. We went down a hallway and through another door into the isolation area. There was a cell about four feet by four feet with padding on the floor and all the walls. Instead of a toilet there was a little nine-inch by nine-inch metal grate in the floor that stank in a serious way.

The two guards had nothing to say except I was ordered to strip naked. After I complied, they just closed me in there. Inside, there was no light at all, except for what leaked in around the edges of the door.

Sunday, Day 12

In the silence and darkness, I could hear the crickets chirping "Suicide, suicide, suicide." My God, why are they saying this? "Help me," I thought, but I could not actually say it.

I lay there with my eyes squeezed shut and my fingers over my ears. The crickets slowly faded in their chorus after a period of time, which seemed at least a few hours. There was a ringing sound, followed by hissing, so I opened my eyes. I was covered in ants. At first I just rolled around to try to squish them. Then I brushed them out of my hair with my fingers and off my face and arms the best that I could. Why were they here?

In the corner near the doorjamb, there was a little patch of light about the size of a fingerprint. I moved my face close to it and indeed there were ants there as well. There were exactly two of them and they were fighting with each other. I lay there on my stomach with my face one inch away from them. The two of them were fighting over something. They were fighting over a little tiny round insect. It was a ferocious struggle – those two ants used their combined twelve legs to get the little one to move one way or another. Then suddenly the little round insect was torn in two. Each ant had half. One walked away carrying the half he had gained in the battle, but the other one just left the dead little half there and trudged away.

I screamed. "They killed the baby, they killed the baby." Then I could not stop crying. While I was crying, the ants climbed into my mouth and went down my throat. After that, I could not stop gagging. I had to force myself to throw them up, so I put my finger down my throat.

The guard opened the door and just said, "Behave yourself." I just sat there, with the ants still swarming over me. No matter what the ants did to me, I would not make any sound.

They were biting at my toes, but it was not too painful. They crawled up my legs into my crotch, but I did not flinch. One of them tried to bite my eyeball, but I just brushed him away. I was quiet, and I stayed quiet for hours.

Then the guard opened the door again and he let someone in. "You have a guest." Then he closed the door and I could not see anything again. There were two of us in a four-by-four padded cell. Who was he? I sat down cross-legged in the corner farthest from the door, while the new man just kept standing.

"What is your name?" I asked. "Bruce," was all he said, and I recognized the voice. I did not know what to say. I thought he was deputy director of a national laboratory. Why would he be here? "Bruce, are you here to kill me?" "No. I just want to talk to you. I find you very amusing, Stan Hall." "You got me fired," I said. "Yeah, you lose, I win. It is that simple." Silence. "That is no fair. You were the one who was stealing from the government." "Har, har, har," he said with a forced laugh. "Thinking like that will just get you another night in jail" "How else am I supposed to think, Bruce?"

"Stan, there is a big, huge, bloated, boatload of bullshit called the federal government. Its purpose is to hand out money to keep people happy. What the system produces is paychecks. You should have just joined in with the rest of us in the chorus of lies, taken your paycheck and then looked around for how to get a bigger paycheck. To get the bigger paycheck you may have to drop one set of lies and start telling new ones. You take it as far as you can. You get inventive, imaginative; you develop theatrical skills. It's good to learn some fake history and fake science to add to the lies. Whatever works, just do it."

"History is not a lie, history is what happened," I pleaded.

"My goodness, Stan, you are stupid. You think we are the good guys and the other guys are the bad guys. Pathetic. Come to think of it, that is why I am here. It is funny just to listen to you. Let me tell you a little piece of history so you can be educated on the subject. Once there was a silly little fat kid who got a college degree and came to Fairfield Lab and tried to shut it down. Fairfield Lab should never have hired him because he was a drunk and a loser and a troublemaker. So they exercised their right to fire him and they did. That is true history. The reason why it is true is because nine thousand people get their paychecks there and they want to keep getting those paychecks. They outnumbered you, nine thousand to one. The truth is defined as what the majority of people believe to be true. In this particular case it was a supermajority. Stan, if you do not understand this, then you understand nothing."

"Little weasels like you through the years have invented words that have no real meaning. Words like 'corruption,' 'waste,' 'fraud,' 'good,' 'evil,' 'compassion.' They are all nonsense. The only words that have real meaning are 'winning' and 'losing,' you fucking idiot."

I looked down at his feet. He continued to speak. "Truth is what the winners say it is. It is nothing other than that. In this case the nine thousand employees of the lab made it an easy victory for me. You are nothing but a loser."

"What about science, is it all just another lie?"

"Science is another part of it. If I am a scientist and I say something is true, then it is true. It remains true as long as I keep winning. If I ever do lose someday, then what I said will become false. But I have not lost yet."

He was saying something like the Latino Studies professor Geraldo was saying. The professor said that Marx was one who had really said it all – Marx was the one who had gotten it right.

"Bruce, why am I here?" I wanted to know. He answered, "If there were no police or jails, the poor would simply kill every person they saw who had more goodies than they did. That would be the rest of us, in case you didn't know. If the middle class even thinks for a minute that the poor are going to kill them, they won't keep showing up for their jobs. Then they won't be spending their paychecks and paying their taxes, which make the wheels turn. So stop acting just like you are some poor person who is going to kill the middle class so you can take away what they have. That is the lesson we need you to learn in this place. If you do not learn it this time, then we will try to teach it to you again."

He became quiet. I had no more questions. The guard escorted him out.

Now I knew exactly what my goal was. I knew I had to kill Bruce to win. I would sneak out of this cell by crawling through the grate in the floor and coming out of the sewage system via a manhole in the street. I would quietly hike a few blocks, looking for a shopping bag or something to cover me. If I could not find anything to wear, that might be a good plan anyway. If I were to carry out the act of vengeance completely naked, it would better satisfy my basic instincts for conquest and victory. I will hot-wire a parked car and drive to Mountain View. In the parking lot of the Kozy machine shop is the delivery van where I can get the pistol. I could then drive to Fairfield and get the filthy SOB with a bullet in the head.

I stayed awake the rest of the night thinking about the things he had told me. The structure of the world is that without police we would kill anyone who had more than us, and take their things. Police are here to protect us from being killed by those who have less than us.

That also refers to the security people at Fairfield, who were there to protect the nine thousand employees from someone who was going to take the whole thing away from them.

Karen also keeps the police around her so she can continue to have more than me, without giving anything up. Bruce is saying that I would kill her if there were no police. That may be a good plan, it occurred to me at that moment. Bruce also thinks that what I want to do is kill my father, Bill, and take everything away from him. Well, I did hit him in the face with a brick. I probably would have killed him if there were no police at all.

God help me, I thought. I almost killed my father. He didn't deserve that.

My concentration was broken by some noise outside the isolation cell sometime after the first hint of daylight. I did not know who these people were. After a while a loudspeaker came on and seemed to be making announcements that made no sense to me. "Cross-check two" and "Station 1 reply." I decided that this was some sort of secret code. This went on for what seemed like forever.

After a while, a guard brought me a muffin to eat, but he did not speak to me. All through the morning there was shuffling and walking in the hall. People were laughing sometimes and it seemed like they were laughing at me, all locked up in this four-by-four cell. I guessed that the guards had told them all about me, how I had a degree in chemical engineering, was at the top of my class, had a good career, and had lost everything and that was funny.

In that little cell I finally decided that the crickets were right all along. It was time to end this thing. After all, I am just a killer who failed even at that. Maybe I could kill myself by pounding my head against the metal grating on the floor. No, that would not work. I decided that I would have to kill myself as soon as they let me out. I am lost.

Finally, after making that decision, I could sleep. I woke up when the guard brought me a hamburger for dinner. I asked him a question. "Please tell me, have you put me in here because I am a killer?" No answer.

The burger had a paper wrapper – it occurred to me that I could kill myself by stuffing the wrapper down my throat. I could roll it up into a little ball and then push it in really quickly. It would have to work or else I would just look like even more of a fool. Maybe this was a test? I thought to myself. Yes, they are testing me, trying to see if I am foolish enough so that I would try to kill myself and fail even at that. I will not let them have the satisfaction.

"Dear God, get me out of this place so I can just go home and die a peaceful death," I said out loud, sitting on the floor of the cell.

There was something about the thought of being dead that was so relaxing, however. I could not wait to kill myself and finally have peace. There would be no bother or worry.

I suddenly felt a deep peace inside of me. It was late at night again and I fell into a wonderful sleep.

Monday, Day 13

I was awoken again the next morning by a guard who said I had a visitor. He gave me a robe and put the handcuffs on me again and we walked out through another set of doors and into the visitor room with the Plexiglas wall. It was my lawyer, Mr. Schultz, but this time he had that lady cop Debbie O'Connor with him. He picked up the phone and started talking. The guard had to unlock the handcuffs so I could converse.

"We have some good news for you, Stan. Here, let me put Debbie on the phone." He handed the phone to Debbie. "Stan, the charges against you have been dropped." "I did not do it. I was framed." She seemed embarrassed. "Yes, we know what you are saying. But Officer Branch, the one you had a scuffle with in East Palo Alto, is a friend of mine. He has changed his mind and it is OK for you to be released."

"What?" I said.

"The court will reduce your sentence to house arrest followed by probation." I was wondering what she was talking about. "What are you saying?" I asked. "You are seeing the magistrate today, and you are going home with us later this morning."

I turned to the guard: "Is that right?" "I suppose so," he said. "I'm just supposed to keep you here for the next half hour while they get your belongings."

I turned back to Debbie and there was still Leroy's blood all over my face. "What happened to you?" "My cellmate was trying to rape me but I kicked his ass." I said with a bit of pride.

I was put into handcuffs for the last time and led into the courtroom for one last appearance. I accepted the deal they offered me.

Debbie O'Connor drove me to my old home on Springer Road. I could not understand why she was doing this.

Along the way, she told me that she had really loved my mother and that she was the nicest person that she had ever met. The police officers from all over the area used to visit her house during the day and stop in for coffee and Danish pastries. They used to call her house the "Springer Road sub-station." Debbie could not stop talking about her. She said my mother had spoken so highly of me: about how I was a top graduate at UC Berkeley in chemical engineering and was doing really well at Fairfield Laboratory. Debbie had understood that something had gone terribly wrong there but did not know quite what it was.

She pulled her car into the driveway and there was a cop car there already. It was officer Randles. He came out with a big smile, as always, "Hey guy, how are you?" – as if nothing had ever been wrong. "I heard that you have been through some, let's say, challenging circumstances lately," he said with his usual laugh. I said, "You are not kidding," staring at my shoe tops.

"This will be your house exclusively for the next couple of months while you are under house arrest. That means you stay in the house and we will bring you groceries. You are not to leave even if you get a job –

for the first week. After that we will make arrangements for you to come and go on a fixed schedule."

"What about my dad?" I asked. "Your dad is part of this deal. He has agreed to let you have the house to yourself to serve out your time. He will go nowhere near the house unless you call him and specifically ask him to come over. There is a mountain of paperwork for you to fill out today. Let me get it out of the squad car."

"Damn!" I said, "Neal you are such a nice guy – for a cop." Then he pointed at Debbie. "She's the really nice one. She's not a cop!" Debbie explained that she was a public safety officer and was dispatched with the police. She stood in front of me wearing a blue uniform that said "Mountain View Public Safety" on the lapel. "You probably never noticed that I don't have a badge or a gun... I help people dealing with loss of life or trauma. It can be especially bad for the police who are often the first on the scene of an accident." I thought of how Rudy had been torn in two – and how she had been there.

"She's really a minister," said Neal. I looked at her. "Yes, I have a small church that I lead in San Jose... that reminds me of something." She went to the trunk of her car and opened it. For the first time I noticed that the car did not say Police anywhere. It only said Public Safety. "Here are your belongings from the jail." She handed me a pair of socks and the Bible, still covered in blood, but all dried out by that time.

Officer Randles said his good-bye. "I will be here tomorrow at 12 noon to pick up the paperwork. Gotta go and catch the bad guys. We've got to crush crime, you know."

I said so long and had some sort of unusual feeling in my chest when he drove away. I wanted him to stay.

Debbie and I sat at the dining room table. She told me that Tuesday was her day off and there was just so much she wanted to talk about. I had the stack of papers in front of me and I looked them over a little. It would take all morning tomorrow to fill them out. For now, I just wanted to hear what she had to say.

She had gotten pregnant in high school and was married by the age of seventeen. Her husband, Larry, was twenty-one and had been out in the bars every night drinking and chasing other women. Sometimes he would come home and beat her. She had tried a psychiatrist and a marriage counselor, but finally asked for and was granted a divorce.

The shame and regret after the divorce, she said, was unbearable. She stayed at home all day watching TV, sometimes drinking herself unconscious. It seemed like the agony would never end, but it would soon get much worse.

Her husband had visitation rights with their daughter Renee. One Friday night he picked her up at the apartment and took off in his Chevy pickup with Renee next to him in the front seat. Debbie never saw either one of them again, because they were killed in a car accident a few hours later when Larry, who was drunk, crossed over the double yellow line on Highway 285 in Fremont and into oncoming traffic. Both Larry and Renee died at the scene.

"Do you know what post-traumatic stress disorder is?" she asked. "That is what happens to you when you suddenly lose someone you love. It is a form of insanity." Then she continued, "I would wake in the middle of the night from a dream where I was in the car with them, trying to take control of the steering wheel to keep the car on the right side of the road. Then I would frantically try to avoid the oncoming traffic. It happened over and over again. I would sit there awake in bed and my stomach would tie into a knot so I couldn't breathe."

"The first grief counselor I saw was only interested in getting me to sleep with him," she said with a laugh. "After I got a new therapist, a woman this time, we used hypnosis to get through the night of the accident all the way to the end. I finally realized that they did not suffer, and that it was not my fault."

I said, "Of course it was not your fault." She replied, "That's what everyone told me, but it did no good until I saw it clearly for myself... so, Stan, for about a day and a half I was 'cured' from my trauma. Everything was fine."

She paused. I looked out the window and there were some birds in the yard. My mom always used to feed the birds in the morning, and I imagined her out there right now, tossing seeds on the patio. My eyes came back into the house and all her furniture was still around us, just like she had left it.

"I am going to open up the French doors," I said. "The house is a little musty and could use some fresh air." As I walked to the French doors, I realized those

127

were the exact words my mother would have said if she were there. Mom was the only person I have known who used the word "musty."

One of the glass panes in one of the doors was broken out and a piece of plywood was taped into the hole to cover it up. "Dad fixed it," I thought to myself.

Debbie started talking again. "Stan, it was in the middle of a weekday afternoon just after this very successful therapy session that I picked up a kitchen knife and went looking for Larry, my ex-husband, to stab him. I did not want to kill him; I wanted to make him suffer. I wanted to stab his eyes out and cut his arms off. The idea of putting the knife into his stomach gave me a rush and such a high I could not have imagined it."

I looked across the table at this beautiful blonde woman, a minister, of all things, telling me she had once wanted to stab and torture her ex-husband.

"Why I hated him was that he *did not* suffer that night when he took my daughter from me. I wished he were alive so I could make him suffer. To make him scream in pain and beg for mercy while I just kept stabbing him. The more and more I thought these thoughts the higher I got."

I interrupted her. "Debbie, my father used to whip me with a leather strap when he would get home from the bar totally drunk. This strap he used was split into nine finer straps at the business end, and each one of the nine ends had a knot tied in it. It was called a cat o' nine tails." For some reason, I started choking up and tears were coming out of my eyes. "He bought it from one of his drinking buddies." My voice cracked as I spoke, and I could no longer speak at all as the tears began to pour out and I began to cry uncontrollably.

She spoke again: "I wanted Larry to feel all of the pain, all of the suffering, that I had been feeling. I wanted him to feel how I felt."

There was silence while I stared down at the red tablecloth and tried to control my crying. I looked up at her and her makeup was running. She looked good anyway in that dark blue uniform with the embroidered lapel saying "Debbie O'Connor, Public Safety Officer." She probably didn't even need any makeup; she was a perfectly beautiful woman in any case.

Then I said, "This is all just payback – to make him feel as bad as I felt."

More silence.

"All that suffering is just a thought in your mind and a story you tell yourself about yourself," she said. "It is always a story of missing justice, a story where the world has conspired to cause you to suffer, a story that makes you very important in the world. In this insanity, you see the only way out is to make another person suffer as you have. You have to equalize the pain. In this insane world we live in, you have a real goal with a definite path. You tell yourself that happiness is in making the other one suffer."

"He whipped me and beat me for no reason," I said.

"In your world there was no reason," she said. "What was his world like? How old was he and what was he doing all day?"

"He was twenty-eight," I said, suddenly realizing that he was exactly the age I am now.

Silence again.

"He was a manager at Lockheed where he supervised a department of over three hundred people. Problems with the space program forced his department to downsize dramatically over a period of a year. Every one of those people that he fired had said in the past that they loved and respected him as a great manager. Half of them, when he let them go, told him they hated him and wanted him to die. That included someone he'd considered his best friend for his entire adult life."

"That was his world," said Debbie. "His job was his world."

I continued, "After that incident with his best friend, he showed up to work in a suit and tie, drunk as hell and covered in barf. They told him to go home for the day, to sleep it off. He would not leave the building and went into his office and closed the door. Later he got into a scuffle with a security guard. They terminated him for cause – meaning that he had no benefits. The only job he could find was working in a grocery store, and that was just because he was a drinking buddy of the owner."

"Stan, does any of this sound like someone else you know?"

"I never drank on the job!" I shouted at her. "It was all a lie – it was all a big fat lie!" This yelling caused such a strange feeling in me, like I had temporarily left my body. I kept yelling, "You fucking bitch! Don't you ever, ever, say that I am like him!! Fucking BITCH!!!"

There was a little dizziness and faintness, followed by a feeling of complete painlessness – of total release.

I floated upwards out of my chair to the ceiling, and I looked down on Stan and Debbie sitting at the table with the red tablecloth. The TV was on the stand near the table, and my mother's favorite chair was there. There was a little bit of dog fur on the chair. I wondered where Cujo, Mom's little poodle, was. The white couch was against the wall, and above it was Van Gogh's "Sunflowers."

I looked down at Stan, sitting there, and I said to him, "only the details differ." He looked up at me, and then I became him again.

Across the table was another soul, embodied in Debbie O'Connor, whose only mission was peace. My mouth opened and I heard these words come out:

"What you told yourself was that you only wanted justice so that you could finally have peace. But all the time you knew that peace was never to be found in that false idol. Peace is with us today. There is a simple, happy way to leave the world of ambiguity and have peace. That is to simply be willing to open your eyes to what is real.

"Just be still, and lay aside all thoughts of what you are and what God is; all concepts you have learned about the world; all images you hold about yourself. Empty your mind of everything it thinks is either true or false, or good or bad, of every thought it judges worthy, and all the ideas of which it is ashamed. Hold onto nothing. Do not bring with you one thought the past has taught you, or one belief you ever learned before about anything. Forget this world, forget your story, and come with wholly empty hands unto your God.

"See that you have given the world the role of your jailer. What could the world be but vicious and afraid, fearful of shadows, punitive and wild, lacking all reason, blind, insane with hate? What have you done that this should be your world? What have you done that this is what you see? You made one simple error: you made fear itself into your God.

"You have lived since your childhood in a jail cell, chained in shackles, facing a screen full of images that taunt you and fill you with thoughts of shame and lack. In those images are fleeting fantasies of freedom and peace that you grasp for, but can never hold. The chains you wear and the movements of the images are so carefully coordinated that at most you can only have a tiny touch as each one of them drifts away.

"All that has ever been required of you was to turn your head around and see that the images were the product of a carefully crafted machine, operated by a madman who is completely insane and motivated by nothing more than fear.

"You have seen your brother, your fellow prisoner, as your 'enemy' because you see him as the rival for your peace; a plunderer who takes his joy from you, and leaves you nothing but a despair so bitter and relentless that there is no hope remaining. At that point, vengeance is all there is to wish for. The wish is that you could bring him down to where he is as useless as yourself; nothing more left within his grasping fingers than is in yours.

"You are given this one choice: continue to stare at the projection and grasp at the images as they drift out of reach, or gently turn and look upon the madman and his machine, with your mind filled with the Holy Spirit, and see it all disappear. At once the screen becomes clean and unmarked – where the Word of God can now replace the senseless symbols projected there before.

"Forgiveness is the means by which the fear is overcome. The guilt, the chains, the shame, the prison cells, they are all gone. The only thing that remains is Sunlight - the Holy Spirit.

"You will no longer offer God your gratitude because your brother is more of a slave than you. Your brother is one with you. Let him lean his tired head against your shoulder as he rests a while. Offer thanks for being with him, for if you can direct him to the peace that you would find, the way is open to you, as well.

"The only precondition for reaching the holy peace you truly desire is that you understand what forgiveness really means. He does not ask that you practice forgiveness, make yourself forgive, or even say that you forgive someone. Rather, forgiveness simply recognizes that what you saw on the screen, projected by the madman and his machine, was not real.

Forgiveness merely acknowledges that no harm was ever done.

"Do nothing, then, and let forgiveness show you what to do, through Him who is your guide, your savior and protector, strong in hope, and certain of your ultimate success. He has forgiven you already. Now you shall share his function, and forgive and honor all you see as the children of God."

Debbie and I then sat there staring at each other for what seemed like hours, but was probably only minutes. Then I said, "I need a glass of water, my throat is dry from all that talking." I got up and walked into the kitchen.

While I was standing near the sink, Debbie spoke, "Did you hear what you said?" "Yes I was listening." "Do you believe it?" she asked. "I don't really know, it just kind of came out... Would you like a Coke?" "No thanks," she said.

Debbie knew about my older brother and how he had been lost on highway 285 in Fremont at the young age of nineteen. Neal Randles had been the first officer on the scene that evening and had tried, unsuccessfully, to save his life. Neal was only nineteen years old himself.

Debbie had been speaking with the Kozumplick family these last couple of days over the traumatic loss of their family friend, Rudy. The Goodman family had hired an attorney and would not speak to her or to the Kozys. Bart was working again at the shop, but was awaiting a hearing on the charge of owning an illegal firearm. She was required to not speak any more about the pending case.

She left that day at about five o'clock in the afternoon.

It being near dinnertime, I went over to the refrigerator to get something to eat. It seemed to be quite well supplied: it had turkey, ground beef, salad makings and even some large chocolate bars. The meal was a relief and long overdue. I fell asleep, with all the food and plates and dishes still out on the table.

Tuesday, Day 14

S ome towels were needed for cleanup the next day. The house seemed so quiet as I searched over the place to find what I needed. Maybe some dish soap, maybe a scrubbing brush. I walked past the rear French doors and, of course, one of the panes was still missing and, as I had said, replaced with plywood. I looked more closely and recognized Dad's pencil marks on the wood, the scribbles like he always made. He had taped the wood into the hole in such a way that it looked awful. Later, when the tape would be taken off, it would probably peel the paint. "He could never do anything right," I muttered to myself. But this time I heard myself say it.

Maybe there was some dish soap out in the garage, I thought. The musty smell of the place was familiar, and there was a pile of boxes in the corner where all my schoolbooks were and also papers – piles of papers from my time in Berkeley – which I would never use again.

Against the outside wall was a shelf of motorcycle parts that I had kept since I was a kid. There was a box of aluminum engine cases, an entire crankshaft, a box of old bolts. There were spider webs on the bolts. It used to be so much fun just riding. Maybe I could get a bike again someday, I thought. Checking it all out, I finally remembered that I was looking for dish soap and there was none. I turned around and, gosh, the place was awfully quiet.

There was a cardboard box in the middle of the floor and on top of the box was an old AM radio, the radio he used to always listen to back when I was a little kid. No one listens to AM anymore. It was made of plastic and had been dropped more than once; it was taped together with duct tape that was so old that it was falling off.

I couldn't find the soap, so I went into the kitchen to the sink and decided to just use water. The dish soap had been right next to the faucet all along. I sat over at the kitchen table, gazing at the peeling linoleum on the floor. I was pointed directly at the refrigerator, which was stocked with all the foods that I had always loved best. The chocolate was Lindt brand, which I had insisted was superior to all else in one of the few civilized conversations that I had ever had with my father since he'd moved out of the house.

The kitchen, and the entire house, was completely silent except for the ticking of the kitchen clock, which was incredibly loud. The kitchen table had a few small stains on it, maybe from ketchup. He always spilled his ketchup there. Now, I thought, would be a good time to clean it. With the dish soap and the rag I proceeded to take care of those stains.

He had always made a mess while he ate, and he loved ketchup on his burgers. The stuff would run down his cheeks and onto the table. He never seemed to notice how much of a mess there was, as if he was just a little child, an infant. My father was just a little boy, like Sean.

All I have done is abuse him. He paid the attorney bills, fixed the damage I did to the house, stocked the refrigerator full of food – all while grieving the death of his wife and partner. I figured that he has no idea how to even talk to me, because all I do is beat him up.

For some reason, I began to think about Bruce, how, as far as he was concerned, I could never do anything right. Seeing as he is so successful at life in this world as we know it, and that I am just a failed engineer and drunk; maybe, from his point of view, his description of me fits the facts, as he sees them – almost exactly the way I see my father.

Debbie was here just yesterday. What did she say? Or was I the one who said all that??

It was something like: "...in our fear, we run away from strength and freedom, which is ours by the unity with our Father. We in truth have salvation the instant we stop making the error that our fearful world is real. Forgiveness is the key by which we open the door to salvation, to a different world: one that is worth living in."

It must have been the hottest day of the year. I was dripping with sweat, and I thought there was nothing to do about it because the house did not have any air conditioning. But looking more closely at the ventilation fixtures, I could see that Bill had installed air conditioning just recently. So I simply walked over to the switch and turned it on. Cool air swirled.

The telephone was next to the switch. It was an old-school wall telephone, just like my dad would have insisted on (of course). Taped to the phone with duct tape was a 3x5" card with a phone number, in his handwriting.

About the Author

William C. Sailor lived almost three decades in the San Francisco Bay Area. He holds a PhD in Engineering Science from UC Berkeley. He retired from Los Alamos National Laboratory in 2010 after 23 years of service, and now lives in lives in Albuquerque, New Mexico. This book is his second fictional work.

Other books by William C. Sailor

Fat Boy and the Money Bomb, Moneybomb Press 2013.

www.ingramcontent.com/pod-product-compliance
Lightning Source LLC
Chambersburg PA
CBHW020138180626
46810CB00004B/1612